THE TREASURE HUNTERS

by

Enid Blyton

Illustrated by BARBARA FREEMAN

COLLINS
LONDON AND GLASGOW

This Impression 1970

PRINTED AND MADE IN GREAT BRITAIN BY
WILLIAM COLLINS SONS AND CO. LTD.
LONDON AND GLASGOW

CONTENTS

CHAPTER ONE

GRANNY'S OLD HOUSE

JEFFERY was sticking some stamps into his album when Susan and John came tearing into the playroom.

"Jeffery! What do you think! We're going to stay with Granny and Granpa in their old, old house!" cried Susan.

"Really?" said Jeffery, surprised and pleased. "How do you know?"

"Because Daddy said so," said Susan, dancing round the room. "Isn't it lovely! John has never been to Granny's, and I hardly remember the house —but you've told us so much about it, Jeffery, that I feel as if I know it inside and out!"

Mother came into the room, and smiled at the three excited faces.

"Yes," she said, "it *is* fun for you, isn't it? Daddy's father and mother are such dear old people, and you will be very happy with them for a few weeks. Daddy is taking me away for a while, because the doctor says I need strong sea-air—and Granny and Granpa have offered to have you till we come back."

"Let me see their letter, Mother!" begged Jeffery. He took it and read it.

"We shall so love to have our grandchildren," he read. "Especially as this may be the last year we shall be able to live here. It will almost break our hearts to leave this old house, which has been in our family for three hundred years."

"Oh, Mother!" said Jeffery, looking up in dismay. "Are they really leaving their old home? I thought Daddy said it would be his and ours some day."

"Yes, we thought so too," said Mother. "But you see, since the War, things have been very difficult, and Granny and Granpa have very little money.

They will have to sell the old place, and live in a smaller house."

"Well, it's a good thing we're going to stay with them whilst they've still got the old house," said Jeffery. "I remember it quite well, Mother—it's simply lovely!"

"I've never been there," said John, who was the youngest. "Last time you and Susan went I had chicken pox."

"I don't remember it *very* well," said Susan, "but Jeffery has told us all about it heaps of times. I'm longing to go!"

"Well, you haven't long to wait!" said Mother. "You are going to-morrow! So I am going to be very, very busy to-day, packing for you all!"

"To-morrow!" cried Susan, jumping for joy. "Oh, how lovely! I must go and pack for my dolls."

To-morrow came very quickly indeed. In no time at all the three children were packed into Daddy's car, with the luggage behind, and off they went! Mother sat in front with Daddy, and the three children were behind.

"You'll love Granny's old house," said Jeffery, as they sped along. "It's the sort of place where all kinds of things have happened, you know—and where you feel anything might still happen."

"Oh, I *do* love places like that," said Susan, happily. "Are there good walks round, Jeffery?"

"Most exciting ones," said Jeffery. "There is a deep, dark wood nearby, where we can go exploring. And there is a river that flows through the wood and makes part of it very marshy. And there is a lovely farm, where Farmer Timbles lives, and his wife—she's fat and kind, and she makes the most lovely cakes."

"We'll go there to tea then!" said Susan, jumping up and down on the seat. "This will be a lovely holiday."

"I hope you will remember to be quiet in the house, and to be kind and obedient to your grandparents," said Daddy. "They have had a lot of trouble lately, and it is kind of them to have you."

"We really will do our best," promised John. "Jeffery, was there a dog at Granny's? Or a cat?"

"There was a dog called Rags," said Jeffery, who never forgot anything. "He was a darling, but he may not be there now."

"You'll soon see!" said Mother. "We are nearly there!"

"Look! That's the wood I was telling you about," said Jeffery. The children pressed their noses against the car window and peered out. They saw a thick, dark wood with one or two narrow paths running into it. It looked very exciting.

The car turned into a drive between two big gate-posts. On the top of each sat a stone eagle.

"We're here, we're here!" shouted Jeffery, remembering the eagles from his last visit.

The car ran up a winding drive and stopped before a lovely old house. It was long and rather low, with very tall chimneys. The windows shone with leaded panes, and the sides of the house came out to form a sunny courtyard, in which walked some white fantail pigeons.

With a flutter of snowy wings the pigeons flew to the roof, and sat there cooing. "Rookity-coo," they said, peering down at the visitors in surprise. "Rookity-coo!"

"Isn't it lovely!" said Susan, jumping out of the car. The old house glowed red in the sunshine, and seemed to welcome the children. It had known many children's feet in the years it had stood, and had heard many children's voices. Now here were more children of the same family, and the house was glad to welcome their pattering feet and to hear their happy calls.

"Granny! There's Granny!" cried Jeffery, and he ran to meet the pretty old lady who stood on the steps to greet them. She was small and round and smiling, and she wore a funny little cap on her white hair.

Granpa came up behind her. He wore a pointed white beard, and had a thick mop of silvery hair. He ran down the steps to kiss Mother.

"Welcome to Greylings Manor!" he said to them all. "It may be the last time we shall welcome you here—but we hope it will be the happiest!"

The children hugged their grandmother and kissed their grandfather. They knew them very well, for the two old people had often been to stay at the children's home. They were fond of them, and were very glad to see them again.

"Isn't it a lovely place, John?" said Jeffery, as he took his brother and sister up to their rooms. "We have been given the two little rooms up in the roof—good! I had one before, and it's so exciting there."

He opened a door. The others went in. They found themselves in a low-roofed room, with latticed windows that looked out on to the sunny garden at the back of the house. The walls of the room were crooked, the ceiling was crooked, and the big beams that ran here and there were crooked too! "It's like a room in a fairy-tale!" said Susan, delighted. "I love the whitewashed walls and the uneven floor. Is this my room or yours?"

"It's our room," said Jeffery. "John and I sleep here, and you have the little room that leads off it. Open that low door there in the corner and you'll see your room, Susan.

Susan opened a low door that came no higher than her shoulder. She stooped and went through it. She came into a small room that seemed like a doll's room! It was almost round, had a ceiling that sloped right down to the floor at one side, and two tiny windows that let in the sun. A white pigeon sat on a small slanting roof outside one window, and cooed softly.

"It's simply lovely!" said Susan. "Oh, I know what you mean when you say this is a house where things might happen, Jeffery! It's like the beginning of a story!"

Susan spoke more truly than she knew. It *was* the beginning of a story—but the children didn't know it yet!

They washed, and then went downstairs. Mother and Daddy were talking out in the garden with Granny and Granpa.

"They don't want to be disturbed," said Jeffery, "I'll show you the rest of the house!"

The other two followed him. It was the most exciting house in the world. For one thing there were three separate staircases! One was the main one, a wide, winding stair that went from the big landing to the hall. Another led from the kitchens to the servants' rooms, and a third, most mysterious, led from a door in the dining-room, behind the wall, and up to the children's room, entering Susan's room unexpectedly from a cupboard!

"How simply thrilling!" said Susan, as she went up the tiny stairway, so narrow and dark, and came out of the little cupboard in her room!

There were old family pictures to see—there was great-grandfather, looking rather stern. Great-great-grandmother, looking very pretty indeed in a blue bonnet, stared at them from her frame.

"She's like *you*, Susan," said Jeffery. So she was. She had just the same deep-blue eyes and curly golden hair.

They were still looking at the pictures when Granny called them.

"Mother and Daddy are leaving now!" she called. "Come and say good-bye."

The children ran downstairs. They hugged their parents, wished them a lovely holiday, and then watched them get back into the car. Daddy started the engine and called to them.

"Be good now! We'll write to you!"

"Good-bye, dears!" cried Mother, and she waved her hand. The car swept down the drive and disappeared out of the eagle-gates. They were gone!

"Our holiday has begun!" cried Susan, and she jumped up and down the steps. The boys turned to Granny.

"Where is Rags? Is he still here with you?" they asked.

"He's out with one of the maids," said Granny. "Look—here he comes! My goodness, he'll be delighted to see so many children to play with!"

He was! He was a rough-haired fox terrier, with bright eyes, a wagging tail, and a black spot on his white back. He tore up to the children, barked loudly, flung himself on each of them in turn, and licked whatever leg or hand he could find.

"You're just the same darling old dog!" said Jeffery, pleased. He patted him hard. "We'll go for some good walks together, Rags, old boy!"

"Woof!" said Rags, in delight, and rolled over on his back with all four paws in the air.

"Ridiculous dog!" said Granpa, tickling him with his foot. "I suppose you'll forget all about the old people, now you've got three youngsters to tear about with! Ah—there's the dinner-bell! I'm sure we could all do with something to eat!"

Indoors they all went, and took their places in the long, low dining-room. Rags lay down on Jeffery's foot. He was just as happy as the children!

CHAPTER TWO

THE GREYLINGS TREASURE

FOR the next few days the children and Rags had a fine time, tearing round the garden, going into all the sheds and out-buildings, eating peas in the kitchen garden, and hunting for ripening strawberries.

When Rags was not with them, Whiskers, the big black cat, sauntered along beside them. The fantail pigeons disappeared like a cloud of snow-flakes when they saw Whiskers—but at other times they were very tame and would come flying down on the children's shoulders and hands.

"This is such a lovely place," said Susan, looking back at the old house, as she went out of the little white gate that led to the kitchen garden. "How I wish that Granny and Granpa could go on living here, and that it would be Daddy's later on—and ours too, when we are grown up."

"Look—there is a car coming up the drive!" said Jeffery. The three children watched to see who would get out of the car. It might be someone they knew. But it wasn't.

The chauffeur got out and opened the door of the car. A very grandly dressed lady appeared, followed by a tall man. They went up the steps to the front door.

The children went into the kitchen garden as soon as the visitors disappeared into the house. They thought no more about them at all—until later on in the morning.

Jeffery was playing hide-and-seek with the others. He had gone into a little hedged garden that Granny called her own. In it she had planted all her very favourite flowers, and here her pigeons came to be fed each day from her hands.

Jeffery pushed his way into the middle of the thick yew hedge. He was sure that the others would never find him there! He stayed there, quite still, and waited for the other two to hunt for him.

Whilst he was there Granny came into her garden. She sat down on her white seat, and looked into her little pond, where white water-lilies were showing.

Jeffery thought at first that Granny's footsteps were those of Susan or John, and he kept as still as could be. But when the footsteps stopped, and nobody spoke or called, he carefully parted the green boughs and peeped to see who was there.

"Oh! It's only Granny!" he thought. And then he got a shock!

Granny was crying! Tears ran down her apple-cheeks, and she mopped them up with a tiny lace handkerchief. Jeffery stared in horror. He had never seen a grown-up cry before, and it was dreadful to see tears rolling down Granny's cheeks. Whatever could be making her so unhappy?

He struggled out of the hedge at once. Granny heard him, wiped her eyes quickly, and then looked round in surprise. She tried to smile when she saw the hot, dirty face peeping out of the hedge.

"Oh, Jeffery dear!" she said. "You did make me jump! Are you playing hide-and-seek?"

"Yes," said Jeffery. He ran up to his grandmother.

"What's the matter?" he asked. "Why are you crying? Has somebody been unkind to you? Just wait till I see them, that's all!"

He looked so fierce that Granny couldn't help laughing, though she still had tears in her eyes.

"No," she said. "Nobody's been unkind. But— did you see those visitors this morning, Jeffery?"

"Yes," said Jeffery. "Did *they* make you cry?"

"In a way they did," said Granny. "You see— they came to look over Greylings Manor—to buy it—and it made me feel sad to think that Granpa and I will have to go. It has always belonged to the Greyling family—and now it must go to strangers. Poor old house—it will not like that!"

"But Granny, have you lost all your money, or something?" asked Jeffery. "Why **must** you suddenly go?"

"We haven't *suddenly* lost our money," said Granny. "The family has been unlucky, as the years went by. First, the Greylings Treasure was lost."

"The Greylings Treasure!" cried Jeffery, excited. "What's that? I haven't heard of that!"

"Here he is!" suddenly cried Susan's voice and she came running into Granny's hedged garden. "He isn't even hiding. Catch him!"

"No, Susan, don't," said Jeffery. "I'm not playing now. Granny is telling me something marvellous—about the Greylings Treasure!"

"Whatever's that?" said Susan and John in surprise. They came to sit beside Granny on the white seat. The old lady went on with her story.

"Well," she said, "the Greylings Treasure was brought back from India two hundred and fifty years ago by an adventurous Greyling—Hugh Greyling. He had done a good turn to an Indian Prince, and the Prince gave him some wonderful presents."

"What were they?" asked Susan.

"There were strings of pearls, diamonds set in marvellous metals, a golden cup studded with rubies and sapphires, and other smaller things," said Granny. "There is a book all about this Treasure in the library."

"I shall read it!" said Jeffery, thrilled.

"Well," said Granny, "this treasure was in the Greyling family for some years, and then civil war broke out. You know what civil war is, don't you?"

"It's a war when a country fights against itself," said Jeffery. "Families against families. Daddy says it's the worst of all wars."

"It is," said Granny. "Well, in this civil war the Greyling family was afraid that their enemies would steal the Treasure. So Jeffery Greyling—yes, he had your name Jeffery, and he was very like you to look at—well, this old Jeffery of long ago took the Treasure to hide it away safely. He left the house with it—and never came back!"

"What happened to him?" asked John, in surprise.

"Nobody knows," said Granny. "We think he was killed by his enemies. But anyway, the Treasure was never found or heard of again."

"What do you think happened to it?" asked Jeffery.

"Either Jeffery Greyling hid it somewhere in safety, where it was never found again—and then died before he could tell anyone about it, or else his enemies took it and kept it for themselves," said Granny. "But I don't think that is so because somebody would have been sure to have seen the Treasure, and sooner or later it would have been talked about."

"Oh, Granny! Do you mean to say that you think it's still hidden somewhere?" asked Jeffery, in astonishment.

"I sometimes think so," said Granny. "When the Indian Prince gave your great-great-great-great-great-grandfather the Treasure he told him that as long as the golden cup was drunk out of by the Greyling family once a year, good fortune, health, and happiness would remain with the family. But if the cup passed out of the family, and was not used by them, these gifts would pass away too."

"It sounds like a fairy-tale," said Susan, who loved magic and mystery. "Granny, did the tale come true?"

"Well, in a way it did," said Granny. "I don't believe in these old sayings of good and bad luck, you know—but ever since the Treasure went, the Greylings have been unlucky. They have lost their money through the years, they have had illness and sorrow—and now, alas, Granpa and I have so little money left that we must give up the old Manor House, and go to live somewhere else."

"Wait a little longer till I'm grown-up, and I'll earn heaps of money and give it to you!" cried John.

"I'm afraid we can't wait as long as that, John!" said Granny, putting her arm round him. "We shall have to go before Christmas. Those people who came to-day have offered to buy the house at a good price, and to take the two farms, as well, that go with it."

"Dear old Greylings," said Jeffery, looking at the old house, with its tall chimneys. "I'd hate to think it wouldn't be Greylings any more. If only we had that Treasure now, Granny! You could stay here then, and needn't worry."

"I'd like to see that book that tells us about the Treasure," said Susan.

"I'll show it to you when you go indoors," said Granny. So, that evening, the three children pored over an old book, in which were rough pictures of the Indian Treasure. The golden lucky-cup was clearly drawn and the children looked at it in wonder. It had precious stones set around the middle, and all down the handle. Someone had coloured the picture, and the cup shone as if the stones were real!

The children could not understand the reading in the book, for the lettering was very old, and had faded with the years. They looked at the pictures of great brooches and necklaces and pins, and how they wished they all belonged to the family now!

"It's the most exciting tale I've heard," said Susan. "Granny, I feel as if I must go hunting for the lost Treasure straight away!"

"Many people have hunted," said Granny, with a smile. "But nobody has found it. No—I'm afraid it was captured by enemies all those years ago, smuggled away, and then sold. It's gone for ever now."

But Susan wouldn't let herself think that. She loved to imagine all kinds of things. "I shall pretend it can be found!" she said. "I shall pretend to go hunting for it every day! I shall be a Treasure Hunter!"

"We will, too," said the boys, who liked Susan's pretends.

"My three Treasure Hunters!" said Granny, with a laugh. "Well, hunt all you like—but don't get into *too* much mischief!"

CHAPTER THREE

ADVENTURE IN THE WOODS

THE boys did not really take the treasure hunt seriously, but Susan did. You should have seen her hunting the next day! She tapped the walls of the old house to see if she could find hollow places, behind which treasure might be hidden. She went into the attics and got herself covered with dust and cobwebs, hunting everywhere in the corners.

"You're silly," said John at last. "All these places have been hunted in for years and years. Granny says there only was one secret passage, and that was the staircase to your room, which was found and opened long ago, and isn't secret any more."

"Children, you really *must* go out of doors," called Granny. "It is far too lovely a day for you to spend in the house."

"But, Granny, we're Treasure-Hunting!" cried Susan.

"Well, you must hunt outside," said Granny. "Go along—out of the house you go, all of you!"

So the three hunters had to go out of the house, and they wandered over to the gate of the kitchen garden. Tipps, the gardener, was there and he waved them away.

"Don't you come in here this morning!" he shouted. "You ate half a row of my best peas yesterday and you'll just keep out to-day!"

"Bother!" said John. "I felt just like a few peas. What shall we do?"

"Let's go treasure-hunting in the wood!" said Susan eagerly. "We haven't been there yet. We could follow one of those little paths, couldn't we, and see where it leads to."

"We shall get lost," said Jeffery.

"Well, we can take Rags with us," said Susan.

"Rags always knows the way home. Come on, Rags. We're going hunting! Hunting! Treasure-hunting, Rags!"

"Woof, woof!" said Rags, thinking that Susan meant rabbit-hunting. So all four of them set off for the woods. They went down the drive and out of the eagle-gates. They turned to the left and soon came to the wood.

They went in under the trees. There was a green light in the wood, very cool and lovely. The trees were so thick overhead that only tiny specks of sunlight got through and these lay like specks of gold on the ground below.

Rabbit-paths ran everywhere. Rags rushed excitedly about, following first one and then another. The children followed quite a wide rabbit-path, thinking it was a real path.

But it wasn't. It stopped at a big rabbit-hole and Rags almost disappeared down it, barking in excitement. The children had to pull him out.

"Well, we can't go down the hole," said John, laughing. "That's where the path leads to. Where shall we go now?"

"Let's go deeper into the wood," said Susan. "It feels mysterious and exciting. You don't know what we might find!"

"Well, you won't find fairies or witches, if that is what you're thinking of," said Jeffery, laughing.

"Listen—what's that noise?" said Susan, stopping suddenly. They all stopped. There was a rushing noise that was not the sound of the wind in the trees.

"It sounds like water," said Jeffery, puzzled. "Oh —of course! I told you there was a river that ran through the wood, didn't I? It wanders in and out, and we must be quite near it."

He led the way between the tall trees. The ground became rather wet and marshy, and the children had to tread carefully.

"There it is!" said Jeffery at last. He pointed to where a dark green stream flowed swiftly along between tree-grown banks. The children went to it.

It was deep, and flowed quickly. Susan thought it looked queer.

"Let's follow the banks," she said. "I'd like to see where it goes."

So they followed the stream. It was difficult, because bushes grew so thickly on the bank in some places that they had to leave the stream, go a good way round the bushes and then come back to the water.

It grew wider and shallower as they followed its banks deeper into the wood. It lost its deep green

"*Look*, *Jeffery!* They are *steps!*"

colour and became brown. It bubbled and gurgled, and in its depths quick fishes darted about.

Then suddenly the stream widened out into a large round pool, like a small lake. At one end of the pool the stream flowed in, at the other it flowed out.

"Isn't it lovely!" said Susan, in surprise. "I wonder how it made itself into a pond. It looks so round that it seems as if someone made it."

"Whoever would make a lake in the middle of a wood?" said John scornfully. "Ooh look—what a marvellous water-lily that is!"

Water-lilies covered the pond. They were of many colours. The wild yellow one grew there, but deep red and paler pink ones lay on the water also.

"I wish I could pick that deep red lily and take it back for Granny," said Jeffery, looking at the one that John had pointed to.

"It's deep," said Susan, looking into the water. "You couldn't paddle out to get it."

Jeffery made his way round the pond, looking to see if there was any shallower place. "There's a big flat rock here," he said. "And another under the water. I might be able to stand on that, and reach it."

The flat rock was green with slime. Jeffery stood carefully on it, barefooted, and then stepped to the flat stone below—and then he felt about with his foot and said, "I do believe there's another flat stone below this one as well. It's just like steps!"

"They *are* steps!" said Susan, in surprise. She had scraped the green slime off with a stone, and below the slime was white marble! "Look, Jeffery—they are real steps. Steps that somebody put here for the pond."

Jeffery stared down in surprise. Susan was right. Jeffery forgot all about the red water-lily and began to scrape the steps.

"Well, why should anyone build steps here?" he said. "You only put marble steps by a pond if you want to feed swans—or go boating—or if you have a house nearby that you sit in to look over the water."

"Swans wouldn't come here," said Susan. "They like more open water. And there aren't any boats."

"No—but there might have been once," said Jeffery. "I say—I wonder if there ever was a summer-house—or boating-house, or something, near here. After all, if somebody took the trouble to build marble steps here, they might have built a little summer-house for themselves as well!"

"Let's look!" said Susan. So the three children began to hunt around the pond. The trees and bushes were so thick that it was difficult to make their way here and there.

Suddenly Susan gave a shout. "I say! Look here! What do you think this is?"

The boys scrambled over to where Susan was standing. She was pulling at some thick ivy.

"Look," she said. "There's brick under this ivy. I believe the ivy, the brambles, and the honeysuckle have grown all together here, and hidden a building of some sort!"

The boys excitedly looked about. It certainly seemed as if the great bramble and ivy cluster might be growing over something. They peeped here and there, but they could find no proper building.

"It's like the Castle of the Sleeping Beauty," said Susan, "all overgrown with thorns. Oh, Jeffery, look, look!"

Jeffery and John looked. Rags had gone after a rabbit, and had scraped hard at the bottom of the great ivy tangle. Where he had scraped, stone steps showed—steps that must lead down to the pond!

"So there *must* be some sort of a building beneath this tangle of bushes!" cried Jeffery. "There must! Steps wouldn't lead down from nothing. There must have been a tiny house of some sort here, with steps leading down to the pool. However can we find out?"

"We'll have to borrow an axe from Tipps," said Susan, thrilled. "Then we can chop away the ivy and the other creepers, and see if there's a house underneath."

"Well, there won't be a Sleeping Beauty inside, so don't hope for that, Susan!" said Jeffery, grinning. "I expect it's just a tumbledown hut built by somebody long ago who loved to come and dream in the wood."

"Jeffery, let's go back and get an axe now, this very minute," begged Susan. "Look—when I pull away the ivy here, there is more stone or brick underneath. I *know* there's a secret house here."

"All right," said Jeffery, who was longing to find out more himself. "We'll go back now, this very minute."

So back they went, making their way over the marshy ground. They would never have taken the right path if Rags had not shown them the way! But he trotted ahead, sniffing, and soon led them to the rabbit-path they had first followed.

When they were at last out of the dark, green wood, they scampered along at top speed, up the drive and into Tipps's garden-shed. He was there, potting plants.

"Tipps! Would you please lend us your axe?" asked Jeffery. "The one you chop wood with."

"Indeed no," said Tipps. "I'll not lend you something to chop off your fingers!"

"Oh, Tipps! We aren't as silly as that!" said Susan. "Please do lend us the axe. It's for something secret and important—something we found in the wood."

"Oh, well—I suppose you want to chop up a dead tree," said Tipps. "Listen now—I'll lend the axe to Jeffery because he's the oldest and biggest—but none of you are to use it except him. See?"

"All right, Tipps," said Susan and John. Jeffery took the axe, and they made their way out of the shed. But just as they turned their steps towards the front gate, a bell rang.

"Bother!" said John. "That's for dinner."

"Let's miss dinner and go and chop," said Susan, who was always ready to do mad things.

"Don't be silly," said Jeffery, putting the axe carefully into the middle of the yew hedge to hide it. "We don't want to have Granny and Granpa hunting all over the place for us, and Tipps telling them he's lent us the chopper. No—we'll go in and have our dinner—and then we'll spend the afternoon in the wood, chopping!"

So they went in to their dinner. It was stew, and treacle tart, and the three children ate hungrily. It was exciting to think of the axe hidden in the hedge, waiting to chop away creepers that had grown around a secret house.

"How you do gobble to-day!" said Granpa, in astonishment. "Now, now, eat properly, or you'll be ill!"

"Granny, we found a pond in the middle of the wood this morning," said Susan, who could never keep quiet about anything.

"Did you?" said Granny. "Well, there did use to be one, I believe. There was supposed to be a summer-house there too long years ago, but that seems to have disappeared now. The river has made the wood so marshy that it is no longer a pleasure to walk there, as it used to be years and years ago. Be careful if you go into the wood very far—it is very boggy."

"We'll put Wellingtons on," said Jeffery. He frowned at Susan to stop her saying any more. So often she said too much, and then their adventures were stopped by the grown-ups before they had even begun!

They slipped away from the dining-room as soon as they could. "I'm going to have a quiet nap," said Granny. "So keep away from the house, won't you?"

"Oh, yes, we'll be far away from Greylings this afternoon!" said Susan. She ran to join the boys.

Jeffery was taking the axe from the hedge. It shone bright and sharp.

"Come on," he said. "We've got plenty of time this afternoon. We'll see what we can find!"

So off they went again with Rags, who was delighted to go hunting rabbits once more. The children did not find it very easy to make their way to the river, but once they found it, it was easy to follow.

"Look! There's the pool again!" said Susan, jumping for joy, and landing in such a boggy patch that the boys had to pull her out. "Come on! Do some chopping, Jeffery!"

CHAPTER FOUR

THE LITTLE SECRET HOUSE

JEFFERY went to the overgrown clump and began to chop away at the ivy stems. Some of them were very thick. He chopped hard above the steps where Rags had found a rabbit-hole.

He hadn't chopped for long before he gave a shout. "Yes! Look—there *is* a house of some sort under all this ivy. I'm chopping by the door. Come and pull away the stems for me."

37

Susan and John went to help Jeffery. He had chopped so hard that he was very hot, and his face was wet. He took out his handkerchief and mopped his forehead.

Susan and John began to tear away the broken stems of ivy. They were more careful with the blackberry sprays, because they were prickly. The honeysuckle came away more easily, for its stems were thin and brittle.

"Yes!" said Susan, excited. "There *is* a door behind here. Oh, Jeffery! Fancy there being a little secret house hidden under all this ivy and creeper—a house forgotten long ago and never used except by the rabbits."

Jeffery laughed. He took up his axe again. "Well, the rabbits must be getting a shock now," he said. "Stand away, you two. I don't want to chop your heads off!"

"Let *me* have a turn!" begged Susan, who was simply longing to chop too. But Jeffery shook his head firmly.

"Certainly not, Susan," he said. "You know quite well that we promised Tipps I would be the only one to chop. I'm the oldest and the biggest, and I know how to use an axe. Goodness knows what *you* might do, Susan, if you began chopping!"

Jeffery chopped hard. Some of the ivy stems were as thick as the trunks of small trees. The roots that these stems had put out held firmly to the door underneath—but once Jeffery had chopped the stems in half, it was easy to pull away the brown roots that clung everywhere.

"Jeffery, we've made quite a hole already!" said Susan, dancing about in excitement. "Oh, Jeffery, hurry! Soon there will be enough room for us to creep through."

"Well, I'm hurrying as much as I can," said Jeffery. "But it's jolly hard work."

Crash! Crash! The axe cut through one stem after another, and at last there was a hole big enough for anyone to crawl through, about the middle of the doorway. Jeffery twisted a handkerchief round his hand and bent back some of the more prickly sprays that the others couldn't manage.

He poked the axe in through the hole. There was a wooden door behind. "I can see the handle!" said Jeffery, in excitement.

He slipped his hand along the door and tried the handle. It would not even turn!

"It won't move," said Jeffery.

"Let *me* try," said John. "My wrist is very strong —perhaps *I* can turn the handle."

But none of them could. It was stiff with the

rust of many many years, and would not move. The three children were terribly disappointed.

"Let's see if we can find a window and chop the ivy away from that," said John. "We could get in through a window."

So they tried to find a window—but the creeping ivy and brambles were so thick that it was quite impossible to guess where a window might be.

Scratched and pricked all over their arms and legs, the children looked at one another and wondered what to do.

"There *must* be some way we can get in!" said John.

"Yes—there *is*!" cried Susan. "I know what to do!"

"What?" asked the boys.

"Chop down the door, of course!" shouted Susan, in excitement. "Can't you chop a big enough hole in the door for us to squeeze through, Jeffery?"

"But do you think we *ought* to do that?" said Jeffery. "I mean—after all, it's a door, and it isn't right to chop holes in doors."

"It can't matter with *this* door," said John, eager to try Susan's idea. "It must be nearly falling to pieces as it is! Go on, Jeffery—chop a hole in it! We'll never get in if you don't. I simply can't wait any longer!"

Jeffery didn't want to wait either. He lifted the axe and chopped at the door with it. The wood was quite rotten and gave way easily. The axe went through it at once. A few strokes, and there was a large hole in the door, through which the children could easily squeeze!

"Good!" said Jeffery, panting. "I say—doesn't it look dark inside there?"

"I guess it's full of spiders and earwigs!" said Susan, staring at the dark hole in the door. "It's a good thing we none of us mind them. Who's going in first?"

Nobody seemed quite so keen on going in after all! It really did look dark and mysterious through the hole in the door. It smelt a bit funny too.

"I believe I've got a candle-end somewhere in my pocket!" said Jeffery suddenly. He always carried a strange collection of things about with him. "You never know when any of them may come in useful," he would say, when the others teased him about them. He felt in first one pocket and then another—and then brought out a candle-end—about two inches of red candle.

"I've got some matches somewhere too," he said.

"Oh, do hurry, Jeffery!" said Susan, always the impatient one. "I want to see inside this strange, secret little house. Fancy finding a house all hidden and covered with creeper, that nobody has been inside for years and years and years!"

Jeffery found his matches, and lighted the candle-end. He held the candle inside the hole in the door. The three children pressed round it to see inside the queer woodland house.

It did indeed look very mysterious. It was full of dark shadows. It looked small, high and round. A bench ran round it, and there was a small fireplace or hearth at the back. A table was against the wall at one side, with something on it. The children could not see what it was.

"Let's go in!" whispered Susan.

"What are you whispering for?" whispered back John.

"I don't know—but it seems funny to talk out loud now!" said Susan, still in a whisper.

Jeffery squeezed in through the hole first. He said "Oh! What's that!" and quickly climbed out again.

"What do you mean? What's the matter?" asked John, half-frightened.

"Something touched my face," said Jeffery. "I didn't like it!"

"It was a spider's web, you silly!" said Susan. She laughed, and the sound seemed to make things bright and ordinary again. "You baby, Jeffery! Fancy being frightened of a spider's web!"

"Well, it didn't feel nice touching my cheek like that," said Jeffery. "You go in first, Susan, if you think a spider's web is so funny! Take the candle!"

So Susan climbed in through the hole in the door, brushing aside the hanging spiders' webs with her hand. She held the candle up and looked round the queer little house.

It had had two windows, but both these were blocked up with ivy and other creepers. The bench round the wall was thick with the dust of many, many years. So was the table. Susan held the candle up and looked to see what was on the table.

"Jeffery, the people who were here last drank out of these glasses!" she said. "There are two here—all dirty and dusty. Oh, isn't it strange to come here and find glasses still on the table!"

By this time the two boys had crept into the little house too, and were staring round in excitement.

"Those glasses are like the very old ones that Granny keeps in the cupboard in the drawing-room!" said Jeffery, picking one up. "She won't use them because she says they are old and rare—how pleased she will be to have two more!"

"Look at the fireplace," said Susan, holding the

candle to it. "There are the remains of a fire there. What fun it must have been to come to this house on a cold day, light a fire, and sit here in the middle of the wood, with that lovely pool gleaming below!"

"Yes, mustn't it," said Jeffery. "I'd like it myself! I'd love a little secret house like this. The squirrels would come to it—and the robins. The rabbits would peep inside, and perhaps a hedgehog would walk in, and sniff around."

"That does sound lovely," said Susan, delighted. "Poor little house—hidden away and forgotten all these years. Let's make it ours!"

"Oh, yes!" cried the boys, thrilled with the idea.

"We'll clear away the ivy from the windows, and let the light through," said Susan, busy planning as she loved to do. "We'll bring a brush and sweep the dust away. We'll clean up the whole house—and we'll make a fire here one day, and boil a kettle for tea!"

"What fun!" shouted Jeffery, and he jumped for joy. A long spider's thread caught his ear, and he rubbed it away. "I'd like to clear away these clinging cobwebs," he said. "I really don't like them!"

"Let's go home again now," said Susan. "The candle won't last any more. It's running down on my fingers now and the wax is very hot. We'll bring candles here when we come, and keep them on the mantelpiece. Let's take the two old glasses with us."

Off they went back home, carrying the two glasses carefully. They whistled to Rags, who had been chasing rabbits the whole of the time, and then made their way through the dim wood. What an exciting day they had had!

CHAPTER FIVE

THE HOUSE GETS A SPRING-CLEAN

GRANNY and Granpa were thrilled to hear about the secret house in the woods, but Granny was not at all pleased to hear of the axe.

"You are not allowed to use such dangerous things," she said to Jeffery. "Tipps is foolish to let you have an axe. You must not use that again, Jeffery."

"All right, Granny," said Jeffery. "But I am really very careful, you know, and after all, I shall soon be twelve!"

"Look, Granny, here are the glasses," said Susan—and she put them on the table. She had carefully washed them, and polished them with a clean cloth. They shone beautifully. Granny gave a cry of delight and picked them up.

"Look, Thomas!" she said to Granpa. "Two of those beautiful, heavy old glasses that we have in my cupboard over there. How lovely! These are rare, now, children, and I am delighted to have them. They are over a hundred years old!"

She put them proudly in her glass-fronted cupboard in the corner of the drawing-room. They were fat glasses, short and very heavy—the children wished they could use them each day for their lemonade but Granny wouldn't hear of it!

"Granny, we are going to make that little secret house our very own," said Jeffery. "We are going to clean it up, and keep a few books and things there. We shall clean up the steps that lead down to the pond—and then, when it is all ready, you must come and have tea with us there!"

"We can boil a kettle on the little hearth," said Susan, jumping round like a grasshopper. "We can make a fire! There's a table there too, and a bench round the wall. Oh, it really is a most exciting little house!"

"Well, I can't see why you shouldn't make it your own house if you want to," said Granny. "Greylings Wood is ours, and the house was ours too—so you can have it for a playhouse, if you like."

For the next few days the children spent all their time in the wood, going to and from their new house, carrying brooms and pans and cloths! Jane the housemaid was quite cross at the disappearance of so many of her cleaning things, and the children had to promise to bring them all back safely when they had finished with them.

Susan took charge of the cleaning, as she was the girl. They all went to the house the next day, and climbed in through the door again. This time they had plenty of candles and two candlesticks. They put two candles into the stands and stood them on the little mantelpiece. They lighted the house up well.

"You two boys had better see what you can do about the windows," said Susan. "It would be a good thing to let some light and air into the house. It still smells old and musty."

"We mustn't have the axe this time," said Jeffery, staring at the windows. "But I could borrow

Tipps' little saw, and saw through the ivy-stems. It wouldn't take long."

So Jeffery ran back to Greylings and borrowed the saw. He and John took it in turns to saw the thick stems, and soon they were able to pull the ivy and brambles away from the window, and to let in air and light.

There was no glass in the windows—they were simply round holes in the rather thick wall. Whilst the boys were clearing the two windows Susan got busy with the cleaning. She tied a handkerchief round her hair and put on an old overall. The house was dustier than anywhere she had ever seen!

Rags was thrilled with the house. He jumped in and out of the hole in the door a dozen times in an hour, and trotted all round the house, sniffing everywhere. He would have liked to live there always, surrounded by rabbits!

Susan removed all the cobwebs first. They hung down from the roof, they stretched here and there, and were grey with dust. They were soon down! Big spiders scuttled away. A robin hopped in at the hole in the door, and flew to the mantelpiece. He carolled a tiny song as if to say, "I'll help with the spiders!"

But he didn't. He flew out again, and sat on a

branch outside, watching the children with his bright black eyes.

Susan swept down the walls with her broom. She swept the mantelpiece, the bench, and table. When she had got all the dust on to the floor, she began to sweep that into her pan.

The dust made the children sneeze. They blew their noses, and then settled down to their work again. It was fun.

"Get me some water from the pool, John, will you?" asked Susan, when she had swept up all the dust she could find. "I want to do a little scrubbing now!"

"I'll help you," said John, who liked to scrub.

"Well, I've got two scrubbing brushes here, so you can have one," said Susan happily. It was lovely having a secret house like this, making it their very own.

John fetched a pail of water from the pond. The children had found that there was a complete flight of overgrown steps leading down from the little house to the pool. Jeffery was determined to clean them and uncover them all as soon as he had finished the windows.

There was a lot to do, but the children enjoyed every minute. The sun was very hot in the garden of Greylings, but here in the wood, it was cool and green. The children had brought lemonade with them, and they drank it when they felt too hot.

Susan scrubbed the floor, the bench, and the table. The floor was of brightly-coloured tiles, set in a pattern, and at some time had had a rug over it, for Susan found threads of it still left.

"I say! What a lovely floor!" said Jeffery, looking in from one of the window-holes. "It looks beautiful now! Who would have thought there was a floor like that!"

It took the children three days to get the little house really nice. At the end of that time it was lovely!

Jeffery had managed to get the door to open now, and had cleared away all the creepers over the doorway, so that light came in there as well as in at the windows. Tipps' saw was not so quick at clearing ivy as the axe, but that couldn't be helped.

John had cleared the steps that led down to the pool. He had torn away the creeping roots that hid them, and had cleared them of earth and moss. They were of white marble and shone beautifully. John was proud of them.

Susan had made the house look really lovely. Everything was clean there now. The brightly-coloured tiles shone on the floor. The table and bench were quite clean, and the fireplace was cleared too, and was neatly laid ready for a fire, with paper, twigs, and old wood that the boys had found outside.

They begged an old rug from Granny for the floor. They brought along a little vase which they filled with flowers for the middle of the table. Susan even brought an old clock that she had found in a cupboard. It had belonged to Granpa, and one of its legs was broken. It had not been worth mending and had been put away in a cupboard.

John mended its leg. Susan wound it up and it went. So to the secret house it was carried, and there it stood on the mantelpiece, ticking away cheerfully!

"I always think a clock makes a house feel cosy and lived-in," said Susan happily. "Doesn't it all look nice? Let's have tea here to-morrow! We won't ask Granny and Granpa yet. We'll wait till we're sure the fire goes all right, and the chimney doesn't smoke. We'll try to-morrow!"

Rags was most interested in the house. He ran in and out, and Susan did wish he could be taught to wipe his feet. He seemed to take a delight in running in the muddiest places he could find, and then walking over the clean floor of the little house!

The next day the children brought along the things for tea at the house. Susan carried a kettle of water to boil for tea. The boys brought a picnic basket full of food. Inside there were unbreakable cups and plates which Granny had given them to keep in their house.

"Isn't this fun!" said Susan, as she put a gay little cloth on the table. "Jeffery, do let *me* light the fire, please, to boil the kettle! After all, I did lay it ready."

Everybody wanted to light the fire, but Susan was allowed to do it. She knelt down and put a lighted match to the paper. It flared up at once. The twigs began to crackle. The wood soon caught fire, and a lovely glow filled the hearth.

But it wasn't so lovely after a little while. Smoke began to pour out from the fireplace, and filled the little house. The children coughed.

"Oh dear! It's smoking!" said Susan. "What a nuisance! Do you suppose we ought to have swept the chimney?"

"Well, I shouldn't have thought the fire was used often enough to make the chimney really sooty," said Jeffery.

Susan poked the lighted wood to the back of the fireplace, hoping that the smoke would soon go up the chimney. But it didn't. It went pouring out into the room. Soon the children's eyes began to smart, and they choked with the stinging smoke.

"Wood smoke is always horrid," said Jeffery,

going outside to wipe his streaming eyes. "This won't do, Susan. We'll have to put out the fire. We can't boil water for tea to-day. We'll have to do that when we've put the chimney right."

"I expect it's stuffed up with ivy stems and leaves," said John. He kicked the fire out, and soon only a few wisps of smoke rose from the hearth.

But it was impossible to have tea in the smoky house. Susan was very disappointed about it. She took the tea outside, and they sat on the steps, looking down to the little pond, and ate their egg sandwiches, ginger cake, and chocolate biscuits there. They drank the water out of the kettle, pouring it into their cups.

"This is really a lovely place!" said Susan. "Look how the sun comes slanting through the trees just there, and lights up the pond. What a lot of water-lilies there are out to-day!"

"There's a red squirrel watching us," said John in a low voice. "Don't move. He's in that hazel tree over there."

The children watched the big-eyed creature. He sat on the branch, his bushy tail curled up behind him. Then with a light bound he leapt to the ground and scampered up the steps to them. Rags saw him and would have pounced on him, but Jeffery had him by the collar.

Susan held out a bit of chocolate biscuit. The squirrel took it in a tiny paw and then bounded into the trees, carrying it in his mouth.

"He likes chocolate!" said Susan. "Oh, isn't he sweet! I'd like to tell him to live in our little house when we are not there. He can be our caretaker!"

As the shadows began to grow longer, one or two rabbits came slipping out of their holes. They sat not far off, washing their big ears, bending them down as they cleaned them. The children watched, keeping quite still. Rags whined, and longed to chase them, but they would not let him.

"We *are* lucky to have a little house all to our-selves in the wood," said John. "All the animals and birds will soon be tame for us, and we can feed them and make friends with them!"

The robin was already very tame. It took crumbs from Susan's hand, and did not seem at all afraid. A big freckled thrush sat nearby and eyed the children warily, turning its head first to one side and then another.

"It looks at us first out of one eye and then out of the other!" said Jeffery, with a laugh. He threw the thrush a bit of bread—but the robin flew down and got it before the thrush stirred from the branch.

"I could stay here all evening," said Susan. "But I'd really like to see what's the matter with that

chimney, Jeffery. I'd like to put it right before
Granny and Granpa come to tea!"

"Well, we'll have a look at it now," said Jeffery,
getting up. The squirrel bounded up a tree as he
moved, and the rabbits shot into their holes, showing
white bobtails. Rags raced after them at once, and
began to scrape earth into the air in a great
shower!

"Have you got the brush here that you had
yesterday, Susan?" said Jeffery. "The one with a
long handle, I mean. I could put that up the chimney
to see if there is anything stopping it up."

"Yes, there it is," said Susan. "In the corner."

Jeffery took it. He went to the fireplace and knelt
down beside it. "I expect there is a bird's nest or
something stopping it up," he said. "It is a very
short chimney, and it should be quite easy to clear."

He put the broom up—and at once a shower of
twigs and moss and leaves came down. It all fell
into the fireplace. "A bird's nest," said Jeffery. He
pushed the brush up as high as he could. Another
shower of twigs and moss came down.

"Go outside and see if the brush is sticking out
of the chimney," said Jeffery to John. John went out
and looked. He came back.

"Yes," he said. "I can just see it. The chimney
should be clear now."

"Right," said Jeffery. He pulled the brush down—but the end of it stuck against something in the chimney. Jeffery tugged hard, but the brush-end would not come.

"Blow!" he said. "What's the matter with it?" He put his head up the chimney and felt about with his hand. To his surprise he found something sticking out halfway across the chimney. This was what the brush had caught on.

Jeffery felt round it. It felt like a box or something. He grew excited.

"I say!" he called. "There's a sort of opening in the side of this chimney—a kind of hidey-hole, I should think! And there's something been stuffed into it—something too big for the hole—so that it sticks out half across the chimney!"

"Oh, Jeffery! Get it down, quick, get it down!" shouted John and Susan.

"I'll try," said Jeffery. "It seems to have stuck No—here it comes!"

B.C.FREEMAN

CHAPTER SIX

A MOST EXCITING DISCOVERY

He had tugged so hard at the box that it had moved from its place. He slid it out from the hole. It was heavy and Jeffery could not hold it in one hand. The box slid down the chimney and landed in the back of the fireplace with a crash.

"Gracious!" said Susan. "What a funny old box!"

"Isn't it exciting!" said John, almost beside himself with joy. "Is it the Treasure?"

"Of course not!" said Jeffery. "The box is too small to hold the Treasure! But it may hold something exciting, all the same."

It was an iron box, with a stiff clasp in front. On the top of the box was a raised letter—G.

"G for Greylings," said Susan, tracing the letter with her finger. "This is an old Greylings box. Open it Jeffery, quickly! Whatever can be inside it?"

It was not easy to open. The years had made the clasp very stiff, and Jeffery had to get a knife from the picnic basket to force it open.

"Shake it, John, and see it if rattles," said Susan eagerly. "Perhaps it might have a few old brooches inside."

John shook it—but it did not rattle.

"It sounds empty!" he said. "Oh dear—I do hope it isn't!"

Jeffery took the box from John, and began to work at the stiff fastening. It suddenly gave way, and Jeffery opened the lid. The three children peered inside in excitement.

"There's nothing inside it at all!" said Jeffery in the greatest disappointment. "Look—it is empty!"

So it was. Nothing was to be seen except the sides and bottom of the box itself.

John was puzzled. "But Jeffery," he said, "why should anyone want to hide a box in a secret chimney-hole, if there was nothing in it?"

"How should I know?" said Jeffery gloomily. "It must have been hidden there over a hundred years ago. Perhaps more. A silly joke, perhaps."

"It couldn't have been a joke," said Susan, taking the box from Jeffery. "Nobody sticks things up chimneys for a joke! Do you suppose there *was* something in the box—and somebody found it—and put the box back again after taking out the things inside?"

"Well, that's an idea," said Jeffery. "But how disappointing for us!"

Then Susan made a discovery. "Look, Jeffery," she said, holding up the box. "Doesn't it seem to you as if the box ought to be bigger inside than it is?"

"Whatever do you mean?" asked the boys.

"Well," said Susan, "if you look at the outside of the box it seems quite big—but if you look, *inside*, it doesn't look *big enough*!"

"You mean—there might be a secret bottom to it!" cried Jeffery, and he snatched the box from Susan. He examined it very carefully—and then he nodded. "Yes—there *is* a false bottom to it. You're right, Susan. How clever of you!"

"How can we open the secret part?" cried John, going red with excitement.

"I don't know," said Jeffery, busy pressing and tapping to see if he could open it. "My goodness! Suppose there is something really thrilling here after all!"

Susan and John could hardly keep their hands off the box as Jeffery tried to open the bottom part. It was no good—he couldn't do it.

He gave it to John, and John tried. Then Susan had a try. But no matter what they did they couldn't open the bottom of the box.

"It's some clever little trick, I'm sure," said Jeffery, in despair. "Oh, I *do* wish we could find it."

Susan grew impatient. She turned the box upside down and banged it with her fist. It slipped from her knee and fell on to the floor.

"Susan, be careful!" cried Jeffery—and then he stopped, and stared at the box. It had fallen upside down, and as Jeffery stared, he saw that the bottom of the box had slid crooked! Somehow or other in its fall, the secret spring had been touched, and the bottom was now loose!

Jeffery grabbed the box. He pressed on the bottom of it, as he held it upside down. The bottom slid away neatly, and the three children saw a small narrow space inside, hidden between the false bottom and the real one.

And this time there was something inside! Yes, there really was!

It wasn't brooches or anything like that—it was a sheet of thick parchment-like paper, doubled over. Just that and nothing more.

"A bit of paper," said Jeffery, taking it out very carefully. It fell in two as he touched it, breaking at the fold. It was very, very old.

"What does it say?" asked Susan, bending over to see it.

"It's a map," said John. "What a funny old map!"

"So it is," said Jeffery. "But what's it a map *of*?"

"Goodness knows!" said Susan. "And what's this one word on the map—just here? It's such old, old printing that I can't even read it!"

"What's that first letter?" said Jeffery, trying to make it out. "It's a J, I think. J—and that's an R, I believe. J—R—there's no word beginning with Jr."

"J—R—is that an E?" wondered Susan. "It's a funny one! And the next letter is certainly an A. Jrea—worse than ever!"

"And then comes an F," said Jeffery. "Jr—eaf—it must be some foreign language!"

"There are some more letters after that," said John. "I give it up! But I know what we'll do—we'll ask someone who can read old writing, and see if they can tell us what the word is. Perhaps if we know what the word is, we should know what the map means."

"Gracious! Look at the time!" said Susan. "Granny will be wondering whatever has happened to us! We'd better pack up and go home."

So they packed up their things, and, leaving the kettle behind for another day, they went to Greylings, carrying the old box with them. What a find they had had!

When they got to Greylings, they found a car in the drive. "It's the same one that came the other day," said Jeffery, looking at it. "It belongs to those people who want to buy the house."

"Well, Granny and Granpa will be busy with them, then," said Susan. "We'd better go into the study and wait till the visitors have gone."

So into the study they went—and, of course, they got out the strange map, pieced it together once more—and tried to find out what the word said.

"If only we could find out!" sighed Susan. And

then a voice behind her said, "And what do you want to find out, little girl?"

The children looked round. They saw that Granny had brought a gentleman into the room—the man who wanted to buy the house. She was showing him the study once more, and the children had not heard the door open.

Jeffery did not want to say anything about the map. He tried to take it off the table—but as it was in half, he only managed to get one piece before the man leaned over the table to look.

"I want to know what that word says," said Susan, in her clear voice. "We've been puzzling and puzzling over it. It's an old map we found to-day, hidden in this old iron box, up the chimney of our secret house in the woods."

Granny looked surprised. So did the man. He bent over the piece of parchment at once. "Where's the word?" he said. "Ah—well, let me see. That first letter is a T."

"T! We thought it was a J," said Susan.

"T—R—E—A—S——" read the man.

"S!" said Susan scornfully. That's not S, it's F."

"In the old days the letter S was written like an F," said the man. Then he jumped, because Jeffery gave a shout. He didn't mean to shout, but he couldn't help it. If the first letter was a T—and the fifth was an S—then he knew what the word was!

But he didn't say it. He tried to take the paper out of the man's hand—but the man held on to it. "Wait, wait," he said, "I haven't finished. T-R-E-A-S-U-R-E. The word is Treasure! How very interesting!"

The three children's faces went red with excitement and joy. "So it's a map showing where the Treasure was hidden!" thought Jeffery to himself. "We can puzzle it out—and perhaps find the Treasure for Granny!"

"May I take this old piece of paper to a friend of mine who is extremely clever at puzzling out old papers?" said the gentleman, suddenly, turning politely to Granny. "I could perhaps find out a good deal more for you, Mrs. Greyling, and it might be most interesting."

"Well—it's kind of you," said Granny, not knowing quite what to do. "But I'd rather like to keep the paper and show it to my husband."

"Very well," said the man, "I'll take it with me now, show it to my friend at once, and send it back to you to-night, with a note telling you what he says about it."

But Jeffery did not want the precious paper to go

out of his sight. "Please, it's mine," he said. "I want it. We found it ourselves."

"Of course, of course, my dear boy," said the man, smiling at Jeffery. "I quite understand your feelings. I will only keep the paper an hour—my friend is staying at a hotel nearby, and will tell me at once his opinion of it—whether it is genuinely old or not—and if it contains anything of importance to you. Your grandmother has been so kind to me that I would like to do her this little service, if I may."

Poor Granny could do nothing but smile and thank him. She did indeed think it was kind of him, but she was sorry because she guessed that the children wanted to show her their find and talk about it as soon as the man had gone. But as she hoped he would buy Greylings, she did not like to offend him.

"Take it, by all means," said Granny politely. "It would be kind of you to find out exactly what the paper means—if it *does* mean anything!"

The man patted Jeffery on the shoulder. The boy was angry, and looked it. What right had this man to go off with their precious paper?

He went almost at once, carrying the parchment carefully in his hand.

The children clustered together as soon as Granny

took the man out of the room to his car.

"What did you want to go and tell our secret to a stranger for, you stupid, silly girl?" said Jeffery to Susan. "Now see what you've done! He's guessed it's something to do with the long-lost Greylings Treasure—and he's got the map. At least—he's only got half of it, thank goodness! I was quick enough to get the other half, and hide it behind my back before he saw it. So he won't be able to tell much from *his* half!"

"That was quick of you, Jeffery," said John. "But really, Susan *is* an idiot to go and blurt out our secret like that."

"I'm sorry," said Susan, looking ready to cry. "I didn't think. I really felt so excited."

"Well, Susan, if that's a map showing where the Treasure was hidden, we don't want strangers going after it and finding it," said Jeffery. "I should have thought you would have been sharp enough to keep your tongue quiet."

"Don't grumble at me so, Jeffery," said Susan, who hated her big brother to think she was silly. "I'm very, very sorry, really I am."

"Well, don't say a word another time," said Jeffery. "We must just wait and see what happens now—I hope the man brings back our paper all right."

CHAPTER SEVEN

MR. POTS OF MONEY

GRANNY was told all about the finding of the
box, and she called Granpa to hear about it when
he came in. They looked at the old iron box with
the big letter G on it. They exclaimed over the
secret bottom, where the paper had been hidden.
And Granpa longed for the man to bring back the
parchment so that he might see the map himself.

"I shan't tell *any*one that we've got the other half

of the map," said Jeffery to the others, when they were alone once more. "Not *any*one. This is *our* secret—and if there's going to be any finding of the Treasure, *we're* going to do it. See?"

The others saw quite well and they agreed heartily with Jeffery. They waited impatiently for the man to come back.

"Supposing he doesn't?" said Susan. "Supposing he keeps the paper for himself, and tries to get the Treasure?"

"Oh, don't be so silly, Susan," said Jeffery, who still felt cross with her. "How can he find anything if *we*'ve got one half of the map? Do use your brains."

"I *am* using them," said Susan indignantly. "He might be able to make out enough, just by using his half. It looked to me to be the most important half."

"Here he is again!" cried John, from the window. "And he's got the map. Good!"

The man was shown into the study again, and Granny and Granpa came too, eager to hear what was said.

"I've taken the paper to my friend to puzzle out," said the man, whose name was Mr. Potts. "He says there is no doubt at all that it is an old map, which shows the whereabouts of some Treasure."

"Really!" said Granny, thrilled.

"Yes," said Mr. Potts, his big moustaches seeming to bristle with excitement too. "But my friend, who is used to dealing with old documents like this, says that there is only half of the real map here. He says there should be another half."

"Dear dear," said Granny, looking round the room as if she expected the other half to come floating down to her. "Now where can that be? In the box, do you think?"

"Quite likely," said the man eagerly. "May I look and see?"

Jeffery gave a secret wink at the others. He handed Mr. Potts the box. He felt quite safe in doing that because he knew quite well that there was nothing in the box at all! The other half of the old map was at that moment in the top drawer of the desk in the corner! Jeffery had slipped it there as soon as he had seen Mr. Potts coming up the steps again.

Mr. Potts shook the box. He opened and shut the false bottom. He peered into the secret hiding-place and scraped round it with a pencil. There was nothing there at all.

"No," he said. "It's quite empty. But I am perfectly certain there must be another half to this old map. Until it is found, no one will be able to hunt for the Treasure. Do *you* know where it is?" he said very suddenly, wheeling round on Susan.

Susan had no idea where Jeffery had put the map. She shook her head. "No," she said, "I don't know where it is at all."

"Do *you*?" asked the man, staring at John. John went very red. Like Susan, he had no idea where the half was but he couldn't help blushing.

"I don't know at all where it is," he said.

Mr. Potts turned to ask Jeffery—but that sharp boy had guessed he would be asked, and he had slipped out of the room. He wasn't going to tell an untruth—but he was jolly sure he wasn't going to tell the truth to Mr. Potts either!

"I wonder if you children are telling the truth," said Mr. Potts, looking at the blushing John.

That made Granny angry. "Mr. Potts," she said, "I think you forget that they are my grand-children. They are all truthful children, I can assure you."

"Sorry, Mrs. Greyling," said the man, with a laugh. "This boy went so red I thought he wasn't telling the truth."

"May we have our map back, please," asked Susan, trying to make Mr. Potts stop staring at John, who was looking more and more un-comfortable.

"Certainly," said Mr. Potts. "Here it is. But it isn't much use to you or to anybody unless the other half can be found."

He gave the map to Susan. "That word is certainly 'Treasure,'" he said. "And I should think that if we could find the other half of the map, and piece it together, there's a good chance of coming across the Greylings Treasure. You were good enough to tell me the old story the other day, Mrs. Greyling, and I was *most* interested in it!"

"Well, thank you for your help," said Granpa.

"May I ask a favour?" said Mr. Potts, smiling very charmingly at Granpa. "If you *should* come across the other half of the map, let me show it to my friend, and he will work it out for you, and help you to find the Treasure. It needs someone very learned in old documents to trace out the meaning of them—and I should be delighted to help you if I could, by getting my friend to do his best for you."

"Thank you," said Granpa again. "We will certainly promise to let you see the other half, if we find it."

"Where did you say you found the box?" asked Mr. Potts, turning to Susan.

Susan told him, rather sulkily. She didn't want to tell him any more than she could help, after Jeffery's

scolding—but if she didn't tell him, Granny would —so she didn't see that it mattered.

"Very interesting, very, very interesting," said Mr. Potts, when he heard about the secret house, and the hole in the chimney. "You are very lucky children! Well—don't forget to let me know if you find the other half of the map, will you?"

He patted Susan on the shoulder, smiled at her most beautifully, and then said good-bye. As soon as he was gone Susan stamped her foot.

"Horrid man! Patting me and smiling at me with a nasty treacly smile! He'd like to get the treasure himself, I know he would!"

Jeffery slipped into the room, grinning.

"Hallo!" he said. "He's just gone! Isn't he dreadful? Fancy Greylings Manor being *his*! I just simply couldn't bear it!"

"He's frightfully rich, Granny says," said John.

"Well, Potts is a good name for him then," said Jeffery, grinning again. "Mr. Pots of Money!"

The others laughed. "You were clever to slip out of the room before you could be asked if you knew where the other half was," said Susan. "John went awfully red. I really thought Mr. Pots of Money would guess that he knew about the other bit of map."

"Where's the half he brought?" asked Jeffery.

John gave it to him. "Oh, good—well now we'll be able to fit the pieces together and see what *we* can puzzle out. We may not be clever and learned, like Mr. Potts's friend is—but I hope we're smart enough to see what this map means!"

"Let's go up to our room to look at it," said John. "If dear Mr. Potts comes back suddenly, he might see we have two bits. And I say—suppose Granpa sees them! He has promised to let Mr. Potts see the other half."

"Well, we mustn't let him or Granma see the half then," said Jeffery. "Now remember, Susan—don't you go and give the game away!"

"Of course I shan't!" said Susan crossly. "Don't keep saying things like that, Jeffery."

"Come on. Let's go up to our room and have a good look at the map again," said John. So they set out to go upstairs—but Granny and Granpa were in the hall, near the stairs. Suppose they stopped the children and asked them about the other half of the map, whilst they still thought of it?

"Susan! We'll go up to our rooms by that secret staircase that leads into your room," said Jeffery. "Quick! Come into the dining-room before we're seen."

They slipped unseen into the dining-room and went up the funny, narrow stairs that wound up to Susan's room. All three children stepped out of Susan's cupboard, laughing.

"It's fun to come up those old stairs!" said Susan. "There's a table in your room, Jeffery. Let's go and put the map there and really study it hard. Now that we know it may be a map of where the Treasure was hidden, it is much, much more exciting!"

Soon the three children were bending over the funny old document. Jeffery hurriedly stuck the back of the halves together with gummed paper, so that they could see everything better.

"Look!" he said suddenly. "Do you see this half that Mr. Potts took away? Compare it with the other half—and you'll see that every line on Mr. Potts's piece looks dented—as if someone had run a pencil over every bit of the map! Do you know what has been done!"

"No, what?" asked Susan, puzzled.

"Somebody has traced the map," said Jeffery. "They wanted a copy of it—so they laid tracing paper over it, and pencilled a copy! The lines would show through the tracing paper quite clearly. It's like when we trace maps at school. Mr. Potts has got a copy of this! No wonder he was willing to bring it back so quickly!"

"That means he thinks it's a proper map, showing where the Treasure *is*," said John slowly.

"It shows something else too," said Jeffery. "It shows that he means to try and find it! Why would he take a copy of it if he didn't want to find it! No—he believes in Greylings Treasure—and he believes in our map. Thank *goodness* he only saw half!"

"Do you think he may try to get the other half?" asked John solemnly.

"I hope not!" said Jeffery. "But you never know. Do you know what I'm going to do? I'm going to take a tracing of the map myself—and then put the real map into some good safe place so that we don't need to use it. We'll hide the tracing too, except when we use it."

"Do the copy now," said John. "I can see Granny and Granpa in the garden, and Mr. Potts has gone. Then we can hide the real map away."

Jeffery got some tracing paper and sharpened a pencil.

In ten minutes he had carefully traced the map on the paper, which he folded and put into his pocket.

"Now we'll hide the *real* map!" he said.

"Where?" asked Susan.

"It had better be somewhere quite simple," said Jeffery. "Difficult places are always searched. *I* know! We'll put the map in your dolls' house,

Susan! I'm sure no one would think of looking there!"

Jeffery got some seccotine, and knelt down on the floor. He carefully stuck the two halves of the map on to two ceilings in Susan's dolls' house—on the bedroom ceiling, and on the kitchen ceiling!

"Nobody, nobody would *ever* think of looking there!" said Susan, in delight. And, indeed, it was a clever place.

The bell rang for supper.

"Now we shan't have any time to work out the map!" said Jeffery. "Bother! We'll do it afterwards, when we're in bed! You can come into our room, Susan, and we'll see if we can work out the map. We'd better wash now, and change into something clean. Hurry!"

CHAPTER EIGHT

WHERE IS THE WINDING ROAD ?

AT supper that night Granny and Granpa asked the children all kinds of questions about the secret house and the iron box. They were really just as excited as the three children.

Jeffery said nothing at all about the other half of the map. Granpa wanted to see the piece that

Mr. Potts had had, and Jeffery took out his copy of it.

"I've put the map in a safe place," said the boy. "You see, Granpa, if people keep handling it, it will fall to pieces, it's so old!"

"Quite right, my boy," said Granpa, taking the tracing. "Very sensible of you."

The children went early up to bed that evening, for they all so badly wanted to study the complete map and see if they could puzzle it out. As soon as Susan was undressed and had her dressing-gown on, she slipped into the boys' room.

They were already in bed. They had lighted their bedside lamp, and their two heads were close together, looking hard at the map.

Susan climbed into bed beside them and looked too.

"It's an odd sort of map," said Jeffery. "Look at this curving snake thing—it must be a road! And then there are three big trees. Well, those trees are probably dead by now and fallen down. But it's possible they may still be standing in a row somewhere."

"And look at this funny hump-shaped thing" said John, pointing with his finger. "Is it a hill? There aren't any hills like that round here, are there?"

"There might be," said Jeffery. "We haven't

explored everywhere yet, you know. And goodness knows what might be in that deep wood of ours! It's almost a forest, it's so thick and so big."

"Then what's this funny little drawing down here?" said Susan, pointing to what looked like a roughly drawn church. "It's got a row of queer little lines beneath it— steps up to it, I suppose."

"It's very odd," said Jeffery, his face red with trying to make out the map. "I read it like this— first we have to go down a winding road or lane. Then we come somewhere where there are three big trees in a line. Then we come to a hump-backed hill. Near there we shall find a little church or building of some sort—and perhaps the Treasure is hidden somewhere about there."

"That sounds splendid, Jeffery!" said Susan, her eyes shining with excitement. "I wonder where the winding road is?"

"We'll get a map of the district," said Jeffery. "It will show us all the winding roads there are. We should come to the three big trees at the fourth bend in the road. If you count, you'll see there are four bends in the drawing."

"Yes. So there are," said Susan. "You are clever, Jeffery! Oh, I'm longing to go exploring now. Where can we get a map to see if there are any winding roads round here?"

"I believe there's one in Granpa's study," said John. "I saw Granpa looking at it the other day. Shall I slip down and fetch it?"

"Yes," said Jeffery. "Go down Susan's little staircase, John. You won't be seen then, perhaps."

John slipped out of bed. He ran into Susan's room, opened her cupboard door, and went down the curious little stair. He stopped at the bottom to listen if there was anyone in the dining-room. He could hear nothing. He stepped into the dining-room, ran to the door and then crept into the study, which was nearby. He could hear the wireless murmuring in the drawing-room.

"Good!" thought John. "If I do make a bit of a noise, no one will hear me if the wireless is on!"

He opened the glass front of the bookcase. It made a click as it ran back. But nobody heard. John hurriedly looked down the row of books. He was sure the map had been put back there.

It had. There it was. "Map of the Greylings Lands."

He took it out of the bookcase, shut the glass front, which made a most alarming click again, and then ran back to the staircase. He was up it and into Susan's bedroom in a trice.

"Good boy!" said Jeffery, pleased, when John danced in, holding up the map. "You've been jolly quick. But what a row you made! We heard the click of the bookcase up here!"

"Yes, I know—I couldn't help it," said John. "But the wireless is on, so Granny won't hear anything. Come on, let's see if we can find this winding road."

They opened the big folding-map. It showed the whole of the land held by the Greylings family. There were the two farms, the Manor House and its grounds, the Greylings Wood, and the roads around and through the property.

"It's jolly big," said Jeffery. "I hate to think of it all going to Mr. Pots of Money. He's not the right person to have it. I bet he'd turn the people out of the farms, and cut down all that lovely wood to sell for timber!"

"Look—would you call *that* a winding road?" asked Susan, pointing to a place called Cuckoo Lane.

"It's not *very* winding," said Jeffery. "And it only seems to have three bends, not four. Let's see if there's a road that winds more than that."

They studied the Greylings map from end to end. They looked at every road, every lane. They even studied the field-paths that were shown running here and there.

"Well, it's funny, but Cuckoo Lane seems to be absolutely the only road or lane that winds at all," said Jeffery at last. "Maybe we shall find that it has more bends than the map shows. The other roads are either straight, or just sort of wavy—no proper bends."

"Well, you see, it's very flat ground around here," said John. "People can walk straight from place to place. When there are hills, the roads wind a bit."

"What shall we do to-morrow?" said Susan. "Shall we go to Cuckoo Lane, and see if we can find four bends in it—and maybe three enormous trees, and a hill somewhere?"

"Yes—that's what we'll do," said Jeffery. "We'll go to-morrow morning—and in the afternoon we'll ask Granny and Granpa to have tea at the secret house with us. It will be fun!"

There was the sound of someone coming up the stairs to the landing outside. "Quick, Susan—it's Granny!" whispered John. "Get back to bed!"

Susan almost fell out of bed, in her hurry. She shot across the room, slipped into her bedroom and jumped into bed as Granny opened the boys' door.

"I heard you talking, my dears," said Granny. "It's quite time you put out your light and went to sleep. You will wake Susan if you talk like this."

Jeffery giggled. He knew quite well that he wouldn't wake Susan—she was wide enough awake already! He snuggled down under the clothes with

John. Granny bent over them and kissed them good night.

Then she tiptoed into Susan's room, and softly kissed her too. Susan didn't make a sound. But you should have heard those three children giggling as soon as Granny went downstairs!

"Susan, I hope we don't keep you awake with our talking!" called John.

"Be quiet, John," said Jeffery. "You'll have Granny back again, if you shout like that. We'd better go to sleep. Well, good night, Susan. I expect we'll all dream of the winding lane and the Treasure!"

CHAPTER NINE

A VISIT TO TIMBLES' FARM

THE next day the children asked their Granny and Granpa if they would go to tea at the little house.

"Yes, we'd love to," said Granny. "We're longing to see it! We'll all have tea there at four. What are you going to do this morning?"

"We're going for a walk, Granny," said Jeffery. "Unless you want us to do anything for you?"

"No," said Granny. "It would be nice for you to go for a walk. Where are you going?"

"Along Cuckoo Lane, I think," said Jeffery. "We'll take old Rags—that is, if he can walk after such a huge breakfast!"

"You shouldn't feed him at meal times," said Granny. "He gets so many scraps now that he's getting quite fat. Aren't you, Rags?"

"Woof!" said Rags, leaping about the room like a kangaroo, excited because he had heard the wonderful word "walk"!

"You will pass near Farmer Timbles' house," said Granpa, looking up from his paper. "Go in and see Mrs. Timbles. She will be delighted to welcome you."

The children set off as soon after breakfast as they could. Rags pranced ahead of them, barking at the sparrows in the roadway. Jeffery had with him the copy of his map.

They went down the drive, out through the gates. The stone eagles sat on the gate-posts, looking over the road as they had done for three or four hundred years. They were so old that they had begun to crumble away here and there.

Down the road went the children, followed by Rags, till they came to a stile. They climbed over it and went across a large field. There was a stile at the other end, and then a narrow path that ran between two tall hedges.

"We come into Cuckoo Lane at the end of this path," said Jeffery, looking at the big map.

They were soon in Cuckoo Lane. It began at two cottages nearby and then wandered away across a common to Farmer Timbles' house.

"Now, it begins *here*," said Jeffery, standing at the cottage gates. "We'll follow it carefully and count the bends."

They set off down the lane. On one side was a low hedge of hawthorn. On the other there was nothing—the common stretched away, soft and heathery.

"Here's *one* bend," said Susan, as they rounded a corner. "Good! But oh dear—the lane looks awfully straight now, doesn't it, Jeffery? It looks straight almost as far as Farmer Timbles' house."

"Well, maybe it goes past his house, after all," said Jeffery. "There may be a few bends we can't see."

Down the lane they went again, passing a duck-pond and Jeffery thought they might call that another bend. Then, just as it came to Farmer Timbles' house, it wound round to his front gate.

"That's three bends, anyway," said Susan, pleased.

"Jeffery, let's just see if the path goes on, before we go and call on Mrs. Timbles."

So they went to see if the lane went on anywhere, or whether it stopped at the farm.

To their great disappointment it seemed to stop at the farm gate! Only field-paths were to be seen after that.

"Isn't it tiresome?" said Susan. "But perhaps, Jeffery, the old map is wrong—maybe there should have been only *three* bends shown?"

"Perhaps so," said Jeffery. "But what I'd like to see is some big trees! It's rather wild land here—too much common—and I can't see any big tree except that one over there by the farmhouse—and that's not really very big."

"And where's the hill?" asked John, looking all round. "The land is so flat here. I can't see a hill anywhere!"

"It's very disappointing," said Jeffery. "But let's go in and see if Mrs. Timbles is anywhere about. She may be able to tell us if the lane ever went any farther than this. After all, this map is very, very old, you know, and lanes can disappear easily enough, if they are not used."

They went into the farmyard. It was a lovely place. Cows lowed in a shed nearby. Pigs grunted in a big sty. Hens clucked all over the place, and from somewhere not far off came the curious sounds of turkeys gobbling.

"There's Mrs. Timbles, with the turkeys!" said Jeffrey. "Hallo, Mrs. Timbles! We've all come to see you!"

Mrs. Timbles shut the door of the turkey-house. She beamed at the three children, who liked her at once. She was fat and round, and her face shone like a large, red, polished apple.

"Well, I never!" she said. "The three little Greylings! Welcome, my dears—I'm right glad to see you all! I was wondering when I'd get a sight of your merry faces. How like your father you all are! Ah, I remember him here as a boy—and a monkey he was too! Let all my turkeys out one day, he did, and such a time we had getting them back."

"Did Daddy really do that?" said Jeffery, in the greatest surprise. He couldn't imagine his father doing anything so naughty. "Oh, I must ask him about it!"

"Yes, you ask him if he remembers Mrs. Timbles' turkeys!" said the farmer's wife, with a laugh. "It was this very house he let them out of! The rascal!"

"Why don't you let them loose like the hens and the ducks?" asked Susan, who felt sorry for the big birds shut up in the house. There was wire-netting round two sides, but they did look very crowded together inside, she thought.

"You mustn't let turkeys touch the ground," said Mrs. Timbles. "If they get wet feet, they're done for! But come along, we don't want to stand here talking about my greedy turkeys! You come along in and I'll see if I can find a few cakes for you, and something to drink!"

They followed her into the sunny farmhouse. They sat down in a great kitchen, whose floor was tiled with old red bricks, so clean that it seemed a shame to tread on them. At one end burned a cheerful wood fire. Bright red geraniums flowered on the window-sill, and cups and saucers with a bright red pattern seemed to flower on the dresser!

"It's a lovely kitchen," said Susan, looking round it. "When I'm grown up I shall have a kitchen like this, and I shall live in it like you do. It's nicer than drawing-rooms and dining-rooms."

Mrs. Timbles disappeared into a larder as big as Granny's study. She brought out some ginger buns, some tarts that were so full of home-made jam that they ran over, and a great jug of something that looked a little like lemonade, but wasn't.

"It's nettle beer, my dears," said Mrs. Timbles. "Nettle lemonade! Made of the youngest leaves of the hedgerow nettles, according to an old, old recipe

that my great-grandmother had from Greylings
Manor when she was cook there a hundred years
ago!"

The children tasted the nettle drink and thought
it was simply lovely. They ate all the buns and the
tarts and were very sorry when they were finished.
They were too polite to ask for any more. Rags sat
beside them, licking up any crumbs that were
dropped!

"I'll not give you more to eat," said Mrs. Timbles,
who knew quite well what the children were thinking. "I've plenty to offer you—but I know you'll
not be eating any dinner if you have too much
now! And what will your Granny say to me then?"

The children laughed. They loved being in the
old kitchen and having such a feast. The farmhouse
felt as old as the Manor House.

"*Is* it very old?" asked Susan, looking up at the
enormous black beams that ran across the ceiling
and in the walls of the kitchen.

"Very, very old," said Mrs. Timbles. "As old as
Greylings Manor. Ah, children, I'm grieved to hear
that the old mistress is going, and the old master.
We've belonged to Greylings, we Timbles, as long
as anyone knows. We don't want to belong to
strangers!"

"Isn't it a pity that the Greylings Treasure can't

be found?" said Jeffery. "Then Granpa would be rich."

"The Greylings Treasure has been lost this many years," said Mrs. Timbles, gathering up the dirty plates. "Many a man has hunted for that, my dears. But it's my belief it went years and years ago. It will never be found now."

"Is the lane old that goes to your house, Mrs. Timbles?" asked Jeffrey.

"As old as the house, I guess," said the farmer's wife.

"Did it ever go farther than the house?" asked Jeffrey.

"No, never," said Mrs. Timbles. "It had no need to. There's no house beyond this one. It only runs between the two cottages down the way, and our farm."

The children were disappointed to hear that. But they did not tell Mrs. Timbles why they wanted to know. They got up to see the young chicks and ducklings at the back of the farm, and to look at the lambs frisking in the fields beyond.

"What's that old place just there?" asked Susan, pointing to a tumble-down stone hut, with no roof, not far off. Lambs were playing in and out of it.

"No one knows," said Mrs. Timbles. "It's been like that for years. I did hear say that there was something funny about it, but I never found out what. There's not much left of it now."

"Let's go and look at it," said Susan. But there was no time.

"We must hurry back," said Jeffery. "We've been all the morning! Rags, Rags! Stop sniffing about, and come along home!"

They said good-bye to Mrs. Timbles, who begged them to come again soon. They hurried down the lane, counting the bends again.

"It's no good, there are only three," said Jeffery. "And one of those isn't much of a bend really. And there aren't any big trees about and I didn't see any hill at all, did you? I looked and looked everywhere, when we went round the farm."

"So did I," said John, looking gloomy. "I'm afraid this lane isn't the right one. Well, we'll have to think again, that's all!"

CHAPTER TEN

SOMEBODY ELSE IS TREASURE-HUNTING!

THAT AFTERNOON the three children and their grand-parents went to picnic in the little house.

Granny didn't at all like the marshy ground she had to cross, and John had to keep putting down handfuls of twigs on the muddiest bits for Granny to walk on.

Rags came with them, of course, quite beside himself with joy at chasing rabbits again. His tail wagged the whole time, and his tongue hung out of his mouth.

"We'll make a fire again this afternoon," said Susan happily. She loved making fires. "I hope the chimney won't smoke this time."

"It shouldn't smoke now," said Jeffery. "It was the birds' nests and the iron box that make it smoke, because they stopped up the chimney."

Granny and Granpa were amazed when they saw the secret house, and looked at the doorway and windows which the children had cleared by chopping and sawing away the ivy and brambles.

"I *had* heard of this place," said Granpa. "But even when *I* was a boy it had disappeared. I remember looking for it, and thinking it must have fallen to pieces. But it must have been overgrown like this, even then, and I didn't see it."

Susan went to lay the fire—and then she stopped and stared. The fireplace was not as she had left it! It had been full of birds'-nest twigs and leaves and moss. But now it wasn't! The mess had been cleared out of the fireplace, and was all over the floor.

"Look," said Susan to the boys. "Somebody has been here!"

The boys stared at the fireplace. They, too, remembered that it had not been cleared when they had left the day before. How strange!

"Why should all that mess have been moved away from the hearth!" wondered Jeffery. "Well—for one reason only!"

"What?" asked John.

"Because *some*body was hunting all around for something!" said Jeffery. "Somebody has been looking for the other half of the map! Yes—that's what happened. They've looked up the chimney—and cleared the hearth to hunt for it, too. And look—they've caught their sleeve on this old nail!"

The nail stuck out from the mantelpiece and on this hung a small piece of blue cloth.

"Mr. Potts wore a blue suit yesterday," said Jeffery. "And I guess he's been here hunting—and tore his suit! Serve him right!"

"Well, he didn't find much!" said John. "I wish I'd caught him."

"I don't," said Jeffery. "He might be rather unpleasant! I don't like him!"

The children didn't tell their grandparents what they had discovered. They quickly cleared away the mess, and Susan laid and lighted a fire in the hearth. This time it burnt beautifully and didn't smoke at all. The children were very pleased. Susan put the kettle on the fire to boil.

They had a lovely picnic, except that Rags discovered the chocolate buns, which John had stupidly put on the floor for a moment. Rags quite thought the plate was meant for him, and he ate six of the buns before he was noticed! Then he was driven out of the house in disgrace, and spent his time pawing in the pool at a big fish he could see below the water.

"I know he'll fall in," said Susan. But he didn't. He wasn't fond enough of water for that!

"Well," said Granny, when the picnic was over, "that was a real treat. I think you've cleaned the house beautifully, Susan darling. You will be able to have it as your own hidey-hole whilst you are at Greylings!"

"The pool is very pretty from here," said Granpa, sitting on a step and looking down at the lilies. "I like the bit of the stream you can see too. It winds in and out beautifully between the trees."

"Yes, doesn't it," said Susan—and then a thought struck her.

It was such a wonderful thought that she went red at once. She beckoned to Jeffery and took him behind the little house. He was puzzled at her excited face.

"Jeffery! Did you hear what Granpa said?" whispered Susan.

"Of course," said Jeffery. "But I didn't see anything in it!"

"But, Jeffery! When he said the stream *winds in and out beautifully*, didn't you think of anything!" cried Susan, forgetting to whisper. "Don't you see? We've been looking for a winding lane—but it's a river in the map, not a lane!"

"Gracious! I believe you're right!" said Jeffery, thrilled. "Yes—why didn't we think of that before? The river, of course. At its fourth bend—goodness, we'll have some more exploring to do to-morrow!"

They told John, who came up to see what the excitement was. He glowed with delight. "Of course, of course!" he said. "We *are* idiots not to have thought of that. Good old Granpa! He gave us the right idea and didn't know it!"

Granny was puzzled to know why the children seemed so excited when they went home that evening. But they didn't say a word! No—this was their own secret, and they meant to do their exploring without anyone knowing.

"And now that we know somebody else is doing a bit of exploring too, we'll keep our secret all the tighter!" said Jeffery, remembering the fireplace in the little house. "Mr. Potts has been to our little house—but he doesn't know any more than he did before!"

"Well," said Granny, when they reached home, "that was a very pleasant outing. You were clever to discover that hidden house, children—it is really most exciting. I can imagine how thrilled you were to find the iron box in the chimney too—and the old map. It is a great pity that there is only half of it."

"Well, the other half may turn up," said Granpa. "If so, we'll let that fellow Potts have it and see if his learned friend can make out what it all means. *I'm* afraid it doesn't mean anything."

The children looked at one another, but they said nothing. Susan longed to tell everything, but she knew she mustn't.

They went up to their rooms—and Susan made a queer discovery! She opened one of her drawers to get a clean handkerchief—and to her great surprise she found that the drawer was most untidy!

"Which of you boys has been untidying my drawers?" she shouted to the two in the next room.

Neither of the boys had even been in the room. Susan opened the other drawers—they were none of them as neat as she had left them. She was puzzled.

"I only tidied them this morning," she said. "Granny scolded me yesterday because they were untidy, and I spent ages putting them nice—now they're all higgledy-piggledy again."

Jeffery came to see. Then he went to the big chest of drawers that the boys shared in their room, and opened the top drawer, and then the next one.

"Look here!" he said. "Someone has been through my drawers too. This is pretty queer."

Susan went into the boys' room and they looked at one another. They each thought the same thing.

"It's Mr. Potts, or somebody belonging to him," said John slowly. "They've been looking for the other half of the map. They guessed we've got it, because I went so red yesterday when they questioned me about it."

"So they came and hunted through our things whilst we were out," said Jeffery. "The burglars!"

"Jeffery! You don't think they've found the halves of the map, do you?" said Susan suddenly.

"Good gracious! I hope not!" said Jeffery. He rushed to the dolls' house and knelt down. He switched on the little electric lamps that lighted the house and looked inside. He gave a sigh of relief.

"No, it's all right," he said. "They're here, safe on the ceilings. It's a good thing we thought of such a good place!"

"Let's go downstairs and find out if Mr. Potts called," said John. So they went down. In the hall they found Jane, the housemaid, arranging some flowers.

"Hallo, Jane," said Jeffery. "Did anyone call whilst we were out this afternoon?"

"Yes, Master Jeffery. Mr. Potts came, and another gentleman," said Jane. "They said they would like to see you children. They were sorry you were out."

"Did they come into the house?" asked Jeffery. "Or did they go off straightaway in their car?"

"Mr. Potts asked if his friend might use the telephone," said Jane. "So I showed Mr. Potts into the dining-room and took his friend to the hall telephone. He was there such a time!"

"Was Mr. Potts waiting in the dining-room all that time?" asked John.

"I expect so," said Jane.

The children ran off. "I bet he *didn't* wait in the dining-room all that time!" said Jeffery. "He slipped up the little staircase to Susan's room and had a good hunt round while his friend was pretending to telephone. He's a clever one, is Mr. Potts!"

"Jeffery, I don't think you ought to carry the map-tracing about with you," said Susan seriously.

"Suppose he caught you and searched you. He'd find it!"

"You're right, Susan," said Jeffery. "Well, I know something to trick dear Mr. Potts! I shall make up a false map, and keep it in my pocket! Then, if he does catch me and search me for the map, he'll get on the wrong track—because he'll have a false map to follow!"

"That's clever, Jeffery," said Susan. "You had better do it to-night—and we'll burn the tracing you made, after looking at it very carefully and learning it by heart! We can always turn the dolls' house upside down and study the map on the ceilings, if we forget anything!"

So that night Jeffery made a false map. At least, half of it was quite correct, because Mr. Potts had seen the half with the words "Treasure" on it—but the other half was a real muddle!

Jeffery drew four more bends in the river instead of two, on the first half. He drew six more trees, a few small bushes, and then something that looked like a piece of bread-and-butter with a bite out of it!

"Whatever's that?" asked Susan in surprise.

"I don't know!" said Jeffery with a laugh. "Just something to puzzle Mr. Potts, that's all!"

He burnt the other tracing, after the three of them

had studied it very carefully indeed, and had learnt it so well that anyone of them could have drawn it correctly from memory. Then Jeffery slipped the false map into his pocket.

"Now, Mr. Potts can find it if he likes!" he said.

"Jeffery, can we go and find the four bends of the river to-morrow?" asked Susan. "I'm longing to do some more exploring."

"Yes, rather!" said Jeffery. "We'll go treasure-hunting again for all we're worth!"

CHAPTER ELEVEN

THE CHILDREN FOLLOW THE MAP

THE NEXT day the three children set off once more
with Rags. They had wanted to stay out to a picnic
lunch but Granny had said no.

"Mr. and Mrs. Potts have kindly asked you all to
tea this afternoon," said Granny. "So I will take
you in the car. I want you home for lunch, so that
you can tidy yourselves and change into something
nice afterwards."

"Oh, what a nuisance!" said Susan. "I don't like Mr. Potts."

"Well, you may like his house and grounds!" said Granny. "He has a wonderful lake, so he tells me, and four boats. He says you can go out in one."

"Oh, good," said John, who loved boating. "That won't be so bad."

"All the same, it's a waste of time when we have so much exploring to do," said Jeffery, as they got ready to go to Greylings Wood.

Rags knew the way very well to the secret house now, and set off on the usual path at once. But Jeffery called him back. "Hie, Rags, old boy! We're not going that way to-day!"

"Which way are we going then?" asked Susan, surprised.

"We want to find out where the river enters the wood," said Jeffery. "I think we must count the bends from when it enters the trees. I asked Tipps this morning where it went into the wood, and he said we had to go down the road for about a mile—then we'd see it under a bridge."

So Rags and the children went down the road in the sunshine. After about twenty minutes' walk they came to a small stone bridge that spanned the little river.

"Here it is," said Jeffery. "Come on—we'll leave the road here and go into the wood."

There was no hedge, and no railing. The children simply walked among the trees and followed the stream. It ran quite straight for a little way and then curved slightly.

"Is this one of the bends, do you think?" asked Susan excitedly.

Jeffery shook his head.

"No," he said. "We must look for fairly big bends, I think. They were very curved ones in the map."

A pleasant path ran by the bank of the stream for some way. Then the path stopped at an old wooden seat, and the children had to scramble along through an overgrown part of the wood for some time.

Just after the wooden seat the stream took a great turn to the left, almost doubling over on it itself.

"The first bend!" said Jeffery, pleased. They followed the curve as best they could, and almost at once the river curved again, this time to the right.

"The second bend!" said Susan. "We're getting on, boys!"

They were in a part of the wood that they did not know—but after they had followed the stream for a little while longer they suddenly came to the piece they knew, that led to the pond by their secret house!

Susan was very surprised. The boys laughed at her. "But, Susan, you must have known that we would come to it some time," said Jeffery. "After all, it's the same river!"

"Yes, I know," said Susan. "But I just didn't think we'd arrive here somehow. Well, there's a fine bend just beyond the pond, Jeffery—that's the third one!"

They scrambled round the pond, and tried to follow the third bend. But it was quite impossible because the ground was so marshy just there that they sank almost up to their knees. Rags hated it. He stood and barked loudly at the children.

"He thinks we're quite mad!" said John. "Come on, Rags, old fellow. Don't get left behind."

Rags ran off round the trees. "We'd better follow him," said Jeffery, pulling his foot out of a muddy hole. "We can't possibly go this way. We shall come to the river another way, and perhaps miss this marshy bit."

So they followed Rags between the trees on drier ground. The dog seemed to know that they did not want to go very far from the water, for, as soon as possible, he led them back to it.

Jeffery stood on the bank and looked up the river, the way they had come. It was almost straight after the third big curve.

"Only one more bend, and then we should come to the three big trees or the humpy hill," said Jeffery. "Come on. It's drier here."

They were now able to follow the stream better. Great beeches grew all around, and the undergrowth was scarce. Some of the beech trees were so old and knotted that they seemed to have queer faces in their wrinkles.

At last the children came to the fourth bend. This was a good one. The river swung round to the right and then the children saw before them a marvellous avenue of trees, planted in two straight rows, with what must once have been a grassy lane between them.

Now the space between them was no longer a lane but was completely overgrown with bushes and undergrowths of all kinds. But it was easy to see what a fine avenue it must have been, for the trees still stood there in their places, swaying in their two long rows.

"Somebody planted this avenue a long time ago," said Jeffery. "Perhaps they liked to ride here—or maybe it was a proper roadway at one time, leading to somewhere."

"The only difficulty is—where are our three big trees?" said John. "With so many trees it's difficult to know which are the right three!"

Jeffery stared at the trees. He noticed that they were not so big as some of the others they had passed on their way through the wood.

"I don't think these trees are more than a hundred years old," he said at last. "So they couldn't have been planted at the time that map was drawn. It's three much bigger, much older trees we must look for—more like those enormous old beeches we passed a little time back."

"Do you think it might be three of those that we want?" said Susan.

"Of course not," said Jeffery. "We want three trees *after* the fourth bend in the stream, not before. We must hunt about the place for three enormous old trees. I only hope they haven't died or been cut down."

They made their way through the trees, looking for three together. Susan came across a great old tree, with such a thick trunk that she felt sure the tree must be about three hundred years old! It had a knotty, wrinkled trunk.

"Here's a very, very old tree," called Susan. "Oh, and look—here's another not far off. They are two of the oldest trees we've seen."

"Where's the third?" said Jeffery, looking around. "These two are certainly enormous—and look, Susan, look, John, there's the stump of a third old tree! In between these two we've found—see? There were *three* trees here once—but one must have died and been cut down. Thank goodness its stump was left to show us where it grew!"

The children stared at the two gnarled old giants and the stump of the third. They were in a slanting line, just as the map had shown.

"There are no other trees in a slanting line as far as I can see," said Jeffery, hunting around. "They are either in straight lines, like those in the avenue, or they are just growing anywhere. These must be the three!"

"Well, now we must look for the humpy hill," said John. "How will these trees help us? Do we have to follow the direction in which they are pointing?"

"Either that—or we climb one of the trees and see what we can find!" said Jeffery.

"Climb up the biggest one!" said Susan.

"I'll climb this one and you climb that one," said John to Jeffery. So each boy climbed up one of the old, old trees. They had to be careful because the twigs were brittle, and some of the boughs were quite dead.

But at last they got to the top. And then Jeffery gave a shout.

"I can see something!"

"I can see something!" called Jeffery.

"What?" shouted Susan, at the bottom.

"A humpy hill!" cried Jeffery.

"Oooh!" said Susan, almost beside herself with excitement. "Where is it?"

"It's in the very thickest part of the wood, I should think!" said Jeffery. "Wait a minute—I've got my compass. I'll set it so that I know exactly in which direction the hill is."

John could see nothing from his tree. His view towards the hill was hidden by Jeffery's enormous tree. He climbed down quickly. Jeffery climbed down too, slipping on one bough, and grazing his knee rather badly.

But he was too excited to do any more than mop his knee with his handkerchief. "It's funny," he said. "The hill sticks just above the top of the trees—and it's not got any trees on it at all, as far as I could see. It's just a grassy hill. It's buried so deep in the wood that no one would ever find it unless they knew it was there. Oh, I say, aren't we getting on!"

"Have we got time to go and find the hill?" asked Susan, leaping round in joy. She could never keep still when she was excited.

"Stop, Susan," said Jeffery. "You make me feel giddy. Well, I don't think we really *have* got time! But all the same, we'll *make* time! We'll have a *look* at the humpy hill, even if we can do no more than that to-day!"

He showed the others his compass. "I've got to keep the needle pointing exactly *there*," he said, showing them the little swinging needle in its round glass case. "If I do, and we follow the direction, we are bound to come to the humpy hill. I say—isn't this thrilling!"

They set off in the direction to which the needle pointed—due north. It was difficult going, for the wood grew very thick indeed, and the children had to force their way through. The beech trees had given way to oak, hazel, and birch, and the undergrowth, untrimmed for years, had grown thick and matted.

Soon their legs were scratched, and their clothes were torn. But they would not stop. It was far too exciting!

After forcing their way through the wood for about twenty minutes they came suddenly to the hill. It was very queer, for it had no trees on it at all, and yet there seemed no reason why trees should not grow there. It rose very steeply from the ground of the wood, covered with grass and bracken.

"Well—there's the hill!" said Jeffery in delight. "We *are* reading the map well!"

CHAPTER TWELVE

RAGS IS A GREAT HELP!

THE THREE children looked at the queer, humpy hill.
A rabbit peeped out of a burrow and popped back.
Rags was up the hill like a flash of lightning and
put his head down the hole.

"Shall we climb the hill?" asked Susan.

"Well, we shall be awfully late for lunch," said
Jeffery, looking at his wrist-watch. "But we simply

must go on a bit farther and see if we can find that church-like place!"

So they climbed up the hill, seeing little rabbit-paths here and there. When they got to the top they exclaimed in surprise. They were level with the tops of the trees, and they looked over the top of the wood, seeing the swaying branches for miles! It was a lovely sight.

They could see no sign of any little church anywhere. They looked on all sides of the hill, but there was no building of any sort or kind. It was really disappointing.

"I say, I hope we're not going to lose the trail just as we've followed the map so well," said Jeffery. "But I can't see any building, can you, John?"

"No, I can't," said John gloomily. "Let's go down the other side of the hill and hunt around a bit, Jeffery. Perhaps the church was built among the trees, and is hidden from us."

So down the other side of the steep, humpy hill they went, and spied around to see what they could find. They found nothing at all.

It was Rags who found something! He shot after a rabbit that had ventured too near him, and when it rushed under a bush, he rushed after it and began to scrape there for it, thinking it had gone into the

ground! Jeffery pulled him out—and then called
to the others.

"Come and look here—Rags has scraped out a big
old stone, as grey as our gate-posts!"

They crowded round to look. They scraped away
more of the moss and creeper, and, sure enough, it
was an old stone.

"I guess that was once part of a wall," said Jeffery.
"What *sillies* we are! That old building shown in
the map must have fallen down long, long ago!
All we shall find will be the great squares of stone,
like this one, that it was built of. Let's look."

They began to hunt, scraping away moss here
and there, and pulling away brambles—and at last
they found enough stones to show where some
building had been. It could not have been a very
large building, for the children found a rough out-
line of the shape, guided by the great stones they
had unearthed round about.

"Well, this was the building all right," said
Jeffery. "The thing is now—*where* is the flight of
steps that led up to it? You remember the lines
that looked like steps in the picture, don't you, you
two?"

They remembered quite well. "I don't see how
there could possibly have been any steps to this
building," said Susan, puzzled. "It's built flat on

the ground. If it had been built on the hill, there
might have been steps leading up to it, as there are
to our secret house, from the pond—but you can't
have a flight of steps if you build on the ground
itself!"

Jeffery was puzzled and disappointed. It was too
bad that they had found everything except the steps!
He looked at his watch and gave a shout. "Goodness! It's one o'clock already—and lunch is at one.
We *shall* get into a row! Come on—we must go at
once. We'll come back to-morrow."

"Isn't there a shorter way home?" asked John,
thinking with dismay of the very thick wood they
would once more have to force their way through.

"Well, if there is, we don't know it!" said Jeffery.
"Hie, Rags! Where are you going? Come back!"

Rags was trotting off in another direction. He
took no notice of Jeffery at all.

"RAGS!" yelled Jeffery angrily. "Don't pretend
to be deaf. Come here! You'll be lost if you go
wandering off by yourself when we're so far from
home!"

Rags stopped and looked back at the others. He
cocked his ears up, and put on a most cheeky
expression. But he didn't come back.

"I'll go after him and get him," said Jeffery,
angry. "He'll make us later than ever."

So he ran after Rags—who at once began trotting off again in the opposite direction. It was most annoying. Jeffery called and shouted, and ran after the little dog, but he still would not come.

Then Jeffery noticed that Rags really did seem to know the way he was going, and he stopped and thought. "I say!" he called. "I think old Rags knows another way home! After all, he's lived here all his life and gone rabbiting in the woods hundreds of times. I expect he knows all the shortest ways home. Shall we follow him?"

"Yes," said Susan. So all three children followed Rags, who wagged his tail, very pleased. He led them through the wood, leaving behind the very thick part, and then, most unexpectedly, came out at the field behind Farmer Timbles' house! It was most astonishing.

"Good gracious!" said Jeffery, amazed. "Who would have thought we were so near the farm? Well, that's jolly good, I must say—we can run home all the way from here, instead of scrambling through the wood. It will be a shorter way to come to-morrow too."

They set off home at a trot, and arrived at a quarter to two, dirty, tired, hungry and with their clothes torn and scratched. Granny was very cross indeed.

"You naughty children!" she said, coming out of the dining-room and catching them just as they were creeping upstairs to change and wash. "Three-quarters of an hour late! You don't deserve any dinner at all! And just look at your clothes—and what *have* you done to your knee, Jeffery?"

"Oh, nothing much, Granny," said Jeffery, looking down at his badly-grazed knee, which he had forgotten all about. "I climbed a tree and slipped as I was climbing down again. Really it's nothing."

"I give you five minutes to wash and put on something clean," said Granny. "If you are not down by then I shall send out the dinner and you can have bread and butter instead."

They all shot upstairs, and soon taps were running and clothes were being hurriedly changed. They rushed into the dining-room just in time!

"Now I don't want you to speak a word," said Granny, still very cross with them. "Eat your dinners, and try to make up for your bad behaviour."

So they ate hungrily, and didn't say a word. Granpa had had his dinner and was in the garden, smoking.

"You will be ready at three o'clock to go with me in the car to Mr. Potts' house," said Granny, when they had finished. "It is nearly half-past two now. Wash again, a little more carefully, bind up that awful knee, Jeffery, do your hairs properly, put on your best things, and be down in time. You had better begin to get ready now—it is nearly half-past two."

"Bother Mr. Potts," grumbled Susan, as they went upstairs. She was very tired with her exciting morning, and would have liked to take a book and go and read in the hammock.

At three o'clock they were all ready, looking very clean, neat and well-dressed. Jeffery had bandaged his knee with a clean handkerchief.

"Now, are we all ready?" said Granny, appearing down the stairs. "Yes—you look nice, all of you. Now please behave yourselves, and don't climb trees or anything this afternoon!"

The children were glad to see that Granny was smiling again. She was never cross for very long, for she was very sweet-tempered. They all got into the car and set off.

Mr. Potts' house was more like a mansion. It was simply enormous, and the grounds were mar-vellously laid out. There was the lake that Granny had told them about, and a few small boats moored at the bank.

Mr. and Mrs. Potts greeted them all very heartily Mrs. Potts was rather fat, and had more rings on her fingers than Susan had ever seen anyone wear before. She had six ropes of pearls round her neck, and bright ear-rings dangled in her ears.

"They must be very rich people," said John to Susan, in a low voice. "I wonder what they want to buy Greylings for, when they've got an enormous place like this?"

The children were told that they might go out in the boat, with Mr. Potts to help them to row. They would much rather have gone by themselves, but it would not have been polite to say so.

They all got into the little boat. It was painted red, and was very pretty. There were two pairs of oars. Jeffery took one pair and Mr. Potts took the other.

"It's quite a way, to row round the lake," said Mr. Potts. "I'll show you some ducks' nests, and a little waterfall we've made."

It certainly was quite a long way round the lake! John took the oars after a bit, and then Susan had a turn. They saw three ducks' nests, all with eggs in, and came to the little waterfall, which was very pretty.

Mr. Potts talked a lot. He tried to be very nice to them indeed. He noticed Jeffery's bandage, and spoke to him about it.

"Hurt yourself, Jeffery?" he asked.

"Nothing much,' said Jeffery.

"He did it this morning," said Susan, who always liked to talk when she could. "He was climbing a most enormous tree—right to the very top he went —and when he came down, he slipped and grazed his knee badly."

"A most enormous tree?" said Mr. Potts. "And where was that? In the wood?"

"Yes," said Susan. "Ever so far in the wood. We followed . . ."

She stopped and gave a cry of pain. John had punched her in the back to stop her saying any more. He knew what Susan was like once she began talking. She never knew when to stop!

"Dear me, why did you stop your sister telling me about your adventures this morning?" asked Mr. Potts. "I am most interested. Do go on, my dear."

But Susan would say no more. She bit her lip and hoped that Jeffery wouldn't scold her afterwards. Why was she so silly as to tell things she had much better say nothing about?

"Well, we'd better be getting back," said Mr. Potts, seeing that none of the children was going to say any more about their morning adventures. "I'm afraid this is rather a dull afternoon for you, after all your tree-climbing this morning!"

But it wasn't so dull after all—because something most unexpected suddenly happened!

B.C.FREEMAN.

CHAPTER THIRTEEN

MR. POTTS IS CLEVER

MR. POTTS and Jeffery rowed back to the bank.
Susan got out first, and then John. Then Jeffery
stood up—but suddenly the boat wobbled violently
—and Jeffery fell straight over the side into the
water!

It wasn't at all deep—Jeffery could stand quite
easily. But he got a shock, and came up gasping

and spluttering. Mr. Potts looked *most* alarmed and grabbed him at once. He pulled him into the boat and then helped him to the bank.

"Oh, Jeffery, are you all right?" cried Susan, who had been really frightened.

"Of *course* I'm all right!" said Jeffery, half cross at the fuss. "I can't imagine how I fell in. The boat rocked like anything and I lost my balance, that's all."

Granny and Mrs. Potts came hurrying up when they saw what had happened. Mrs. Potts was dreadfully upset.

"Oh, my dear boy, you are so wet!" she cried. "Come along in at once and take your wet things off. Mr. Potts has some shorts you can have, and a vest and pullover. Dear, dear, I *am* sorry this has happened."

"Now don't get upset, my dear," said Mr. Potts to his wife. "*I'll* see to the boy. He won't be any the worse for his wetting, and I can easily get him dry clothing. Come along, Jeffery—we'll see what we can do for you."

Susan and John went with Jeffery. Mrs. Potts sank down on a garden-seat, looking quite pale. Granny found that she had to comfort her, because she really looked as if she would burst into tears!

"Such a thing to happen!" she kept saying. "Such a thing to happen!"

Mr. Potts took the children into an enormous kitchen, where three maids were at work. They were astonished to see the children with Mr. Potts, but at once saw what had happened.

"I'll take his wet clothes off, sir," said a kindly faced cook, bustling forward.

"No thank you," said Jeffery firmly. "I can take them off myself. I hope I shan't make your kitchen floor too wet, though."

He stripped off his wet clothes, and took the big warm towel that Mr. Potts offered him. It wasn't long before he was quite dry. Mr. Potts picked up the wet clothes and went through the door with them. "I'll get you some dry ones," he said.

"Oh, sir! Let *me* take the clothes!" cried the house-parlourmaid, running after him. "I'll dry them and press them."

But Mr. Potts took no notice of her and disappeared quickly. The cook went to the scullery, and the third maid went into the garden. The house-parlourmaid followed Mr. Potts after a minute, and the children found themselves alone.

"Jeffery! You *were* a silly!" whispered Susan. "It's the first time you've ever fallen out of a boat!"

"And so would *you* fall out if the boat was rocked violently just as you were standing on one foot, ready to step out," answered Jeffery crossly. "That boat was rocked on purpose—by Mr. Potts. He *wanted* me to fall in the water!"

"Oh, Jeffery! But why?" asked Susan, horrified.

"So that I would have to change my wet clothes under his eyes—and he could take them away—and run through my pockets to see if he could find any signs of the *map*!" said Jeffery.

The other two stared at him in silence. They hadn't for one moment thought of such a thing—but now they saw that it was very likely to be true. After all, the clothes had been whisked off by Mr. Potts, although it was the maid's job to take them and dry them.

"But, Jeffery——" said John, beginning to giggle, "you had the false map in your pocket—the one we made up!"

"I know that," said Jeffery with a laugh. He pulled the big towel round him more closely. "Old Pots of Money will have to use his brains to work out *that* map, won't he!"

"What a good thing you didn't have the proper tracing in your pocket," began Susan. But Jeffery nudged her, for he had heard footsteps. The house-parlourmaid came back with some dry clothes—

some rather big shorts belonging to Mr. Potts, a vest, and a yellow pullover.

"Has Mr. Potts got my wet clothes?" asked Jeffery.

"Yes, he has," said the maid rather indignantly. "He won't let me hang them out, he's doing them himself!"

Jeffery winked at the others. "Well, I've no doubt he has some good reason for seeing to them himself," he said. The others giggled. They knew what Jeffery meant. But the maid didn't, and she looked annoyed. She tossed her head, sniffed, and went to join the cook in the scullery.

Jeffery felt rather odd in his big clothes. Granny laughed when she saw him. Mrs. Potts patted him kindly and said, "Well, I expect you'd all like some tea now. I can see Edith bringing it out on the terrace. Come along."

They went to the magnificent terrace that overlooked the lake—and there, set out on low tables, was the most scrumptious tea that the children had ever seen.

There were great ripe strawberries, and rich cream. There were the most exciting sandwiches imaginable, honey in the comb, looking like golden syrup, a chocolate cake as big as a Christmas cake, little iced cakes of all kinds, a jam sandwich stuffed with cream as well, and a dish of the most exciting biscuits. And, to end up with, the maid brought out a tray full of strawberry and vanilla ice-creams.

"Well, this was worth falling into the pond for," said Jeffery, as he ate his second ice-cream, and wished that he could manage a third.

"I'm so glad you enjoyed your tea," said Mrs. Potts, who had eaten just as much as the children. Susan thought it wasn't surprising that she was so fat, if she ate gorgeous teas like this every day. She wished she could have tea like that every day herself—but Granny would say it wasn't good for her, she knew!

The car came round for them after tea and they said good-bye and thank you, and got into it. Mr. Potts promised to send Jeffrey's clothes back the next day.

"That will just give him nice time to dry our false map and copy it out!" said Jeffery, with a grin, as they sat in the car waiting for Granny to finish saying good-bye.

They drove home, feeling rather full up. Granny gave a sigh as they turned in at their stone gateposts. "Dear old Greylings Manor!" she said, as the beautiful old house came in sight. "I am sorry to think you will soon no longer be ours. Mr. Potts will be your master instead!"

"What does old Pots of Money want to buy your house for, Granny?" asked Jeffery. "His own is far bigger and grander."

"Jeffery! Don't call him that!" said Granny, looking half-shocked and half-amused. "You must call people by their right names."

"Well it *is* his right name," said Jeffery. "He *has* got pots of money, hasn't he?"

"Yes—I suppose he has," said Granny. "He doesn't want Greylings Manor for himself though— he wants it for his daughter, who is soon getting married."

They swept up to the steps and jumped out. "Now you'd better go and do something quiet," said Granny. "After that enormous tea you won't want to climb trees or run races, I hope. And if you don't come to supper, I shall quite understand. I am sure you can't possibly manage any more to eat to-day!"

But, dear me, by the time that supper was on the table, the children were quite ready for it! Granny seemed very surprised indeed, but she gave them just as big helpings as usual.

The next day a parcel arrived for Jeffery from Mr. Potts. It was his clothes, all dry now, and neatly pressed. He ran his hands through his pockets. Everything was there—string, handkerchief, two bits of toffee, an unusual stone he had picked up, a pencil stump, a broken rubber, a notebook—and the map! Yes, that was there as well.

"Carefully copied, I'm quite sure!" said Jeffery, putting it back again with a grin. "Well, Mr. Potts may be smart—but we're smarter! I didn't guess he'd get me into the lake—but we were ready for him, anyway. We did that map just in time for him!"

"I wish to-morrow would come quickly," said Susan. "I do want to hunt round that ruined building again—what's left of it! I simply can't *think* why there are those steps shown on the map, if there are none to be seen by the building."

"Perhaps they are not steps," said Jeffery.

"Well, what else can they be?" asked John.

"I can't think!" said Jeffery, frowning. "No—they *must* be steps. But yet there never, never could have been steps there, if the building was set on the level ground, as it seems to have been."

John was thinking hard. He looked up. "I suppose, Jeffery, there couldn't have been steps leading underground from the building, could there?" he asked. "You know—steps going down to a cellar, or something, from *in*side the building?"

Susan and Jeffery stared at John in surprise. Then Jeffery smacked his hand down on a nearby table.

"Of course!" he said. "Of course! *That's* what we've got to look for! Steps going *down* from the building—not steps going *up* to it! Good for you, John!"

"To-morrow we'll take forks and spades, said John excitedly. "We'll probe all over the ground and see if we can uncover a floor of some sort. And then we'll see if there are any signs of steps going underground!"

"Now I shan't be able to go to sleep to-night!" said Susan, her eyes shining. "I shall keep on and on thinking of to-morrow!"

But she did go to sleep, and she dreamt of finding a wonderful place where beautiful treasures were stored—but just as she was going to take what she wanted, Mr. Potts popped up and drove her away! Susan woke up with a jump, feeling very angry with Mr. Potts.

CHAPTER FOURTEEN

A THRILLING MORNING

THE next morning Jeffery went to ask Tipps to len[d]
him a garden fork and two spades.

"I got into trouble over lending you the axe,"
said Tipps. "I don't think I'd better lend you any
thing else."

"Oh, go on, Tipps, please do," begged John. H[e]
saw Granny in the distance and called to he[r]

"Granny! May we borrow some gardening tools, please? Tipps says he had better not lend them to us."

"Well, so long as it's not an axe or a scythe," said Granny. "I'm glad to hear you want to do some gardening!"

"Dear old Granny's got remarkable hearing," said Jeffery. "Nobody said a word about doing any gardening! Anyway, Tipps, let us have the things we want, now that Granny says we can."

They marched off with the tools, hoping that Granny wouldn't call them and ask where they were going to garden. Jeffery slipped indoors for his torch. He thought that if they *did* find steps going underground, they would want a little light to see them!

"We'll go the short way," said Jeffery. "We won't scramble all through the wood again. Where's Rags? Hie, Rags, come on—you can take us the way you took us yesterday!"

As they marched down the drive to the gates, Mr. Potts's car came in. Mr. Potts saw the children and stopped the car.

"I just came to ask if Jeffery was all right after him wetting yesterday," he called, showing all his white teeth in a wide smile. "But I see you are, Jeffery. Dear me, wherever are you going with those spades and forks?"

The children couldn't think what to say. Then Jeffery spoke up.

"We're going to the farm," he said. This was quite true. They had to pass the farm—and they meant to call in for a moment to see Mrs. Timbles.

"Oh! You're going to help the farmer, are you?" said Mr. Potts. This wasn't exactly a question, so nobody answered it. But John, of course, went as red as a tomato. He always did if he felt awkward or guilty about anything. Mr. Potts noticed his red face at once.

"Have you found the other piece of that map?" he said suddenly.

Now this was a very difficult question to answer. If Jeffery said yes, Mr. Potts would ask him for it and would see that it was different from the copy he had found in Jeffery's pocket. If he said no, it was an untruth, and Jeffery, like the others, hated untruths.

The three stared at Mr. Potts, quite tongue-tied—and then Rags saved them! He suddenly saw a stray hen and barked loudly at it. He rushed at it, and the frightened creature fluttered into the hedge.

"Excuse us, sir—we must rescue the hen!" cried Jeffery gladly, and he darted off. The others went too and left Mr. Potts in his car, looking annoyed.

"Quick, Rags, scare the old hen through the

hedge," whispered John, "then we can squeeze through after it and disappear!"

Rags was delighted to find that for a change the children were encouraging him to bark at a hen, instead of scolding him for it. He went completely mad, barked his head almost off, leapt round like a kangaroo, and made the hen almost faint with fear. The children made as much noise as they could, too, shouting to the hen and to one another, as they pretended to shoo away Rags and catch the poor hen.

They squeezed through the hedge, and although they could hear Mr. Potts calling to them, they took no notice and shouted all the more loudly. At last they began to giggle. Jeffery hurriedly picked up the hen, and tore off with it, afraid that Mr. Potts would leave the car and come after them.

But he didn't. They heard the car going up the drive. Jeffery set the hen down when he came to the hen-run, and it ran to join the others, squawking out its adventures at the top of its voice. Rags barked joyfully. He had had a wonderful time.

"Poor old hen!" said Susan, sorry for the clucking bird. "But it did save us from a very awkward moment, Jeffery."

"It did," said Jeffery. "Come on. We'd better slip off quickly before old Pots of Money catches us again."

So once more they set off, this time without anyone stopping them. They came to Farmer Timbles' house, and stopped for a few minutes to talk to Mrs. Timbles. She was most astonished to see their spades and forks.

"What in the world are you going to do?" she asked.

"It's a secret, Mrs. Timbles!" said John. "We'll tell you all about it one day."

"All right, I'll wait till then!" said the farmer's wife. "Would you like some of my new cakes?"

"Well, if you'd let us take a few with us, we'd be *very* pleased," said Jeffery. "But we can't stop long to-day, because we have a busy morning in front of us!"

"I'll pop some into a bag for you," said Mrs. Timbles kindly, and she did. The children were thrilled when they saw her put at least twelve cakes into the bag for them.

They set off again with Rags, who was very much interested in the bag of cakes. Jeffery sent him on in front, hoping that he would be sensible enough to take them the way they had come yesterday.

He did take them the right way. He was a very clever dog, and loved trying to read the children's thoughts. He trotted ahead, and it was not long before the children came to the humpy hill, and found the place where they had uncovered so many old grey stones the day before.

"Now the thing to do is to jab about with the fork and see what we can feel underneath all this moss and stuff growing on what must have been the floor of the building," said Jeffery. So, taking the long-pronged fork, he began to jab strongly here and there.

Each time he jabbed, the fork struck something hard. He stopped, and looked at the others. "There must be a proper floor all underneath here," he said. "A tiled floor perhaps, like our secret house has. We'll clear it if we can."

Jeffery was right. Under the moss, the grass and the bracken was a tiled floor. The tiles were small, and even after so many years were still bright in colour. Rags helped as much as he could, scraping away with his feet in excitement.

After a great deal of hard work the children had most of the floor uncovered. Many of the tiles were broken. Some were missing altogether.

Then John uncovered a flat slab of stone, quite different from the coloured tiles.

"Look!" he said. "Here's something different. A big slab of stone—and it's got some old pattern on it."

Susan and Jeffery came beside John to see what the pattern was. Jeffery gave a shout.

"Don't you know what the pattern is, sillies? It's the Greylings eagle—just like the ones on the gate-posts, only flat instead of rounded. That shows this was a Greylings building."

"Why do you suppose they laid a flat stone here suddenly, in the middle of the coloured tiles?" asked John. "It seems odd to me."

"It *is* odd," said Jeffery, "But I bet I can explain the oddness! I guess there's the flight of steps underneath that slab!"

"Oooh, really?" said Susan and John in delight. "Goody!"

"The thing is—how are we going to get it up to see?" wondered Jeffery. "It looks jolly heavy. I wonder if there's an iron ring or anything that we can pull it up by? Let's clear the whole slab properly and see."

They cleared it from end to end—but not a sign of any iron ring was to be seen. Jeffery stood on the slab and jumped on it to see if he could make it move.

The slab moved at once. There was a creaking, cracking noise as if something underneath was breaking, and Jeffery leapt off the slab in alarm. The children stared at it. Something below the slab of stone had given way, and it was lying all crooked, a little below the surface of the ground.

"Now what did it do that for?" said Jeffery. "It did give me a shock when it moved like that—and did you hear that funny breaking noise?"

"Perhaps, Jeffery, the stone is placed on wooden supports or something," said John. "And maybe they have rotted with the years, and when you jumped on the stone, the wood cracked and gave way."

"I think you're right," said Jeffery, kicking at the stone with his foot. "I don't like to tread on it again. I wonder how we could move it?"

"There's a big stone over there, that was once part of the wall," said John. "I think we could all three carry it between us—then we could drop it down on the slab and see if that would move it!"

"Good idea," said Jeffery. They went to the big square stone and with great difficulty lifted it up. They staggered with it to the slab, and then, at a word from Jeffery, dropped it right on to the flat stone.

The result was most startling. The heavy stone struck the slab, which at once gave way, and, with a crash, it disappeared entirely, taking the heavy stone with it! The children found themselves staring into a big black hole!

"Golly!" said Jeffery, in the greatest astonishment. "Look at that!"

"The flight of steps must be down there," said John excitedly. He bent over to see. Jeffery took out his little torch and flashed it downwards into the hole.

It was a deep hole, with an old stairway leading downwards. "So we were right!" said Jeffery, in delight. "John! Susan! Down there is where the Greylings Treasure is hidden! I'm sure of it!"

Susan was so excited that she almost fell down the hole. Jeffery pulled her back. "Don't be silly," he said. "The whole place is rotten with age—if you miss your step you'll crash down there and hurt yourself. Look—can you see the slab of stone right down there, on the floor and the other stone beside it?"

Yes, they could see them both. They examined the entrance too, where the slab had been, and saw that the flat stone had rested on wood, which, as John had said, had become rotten, and had given way when Jeffery jumped on the stone.

"I want to go down the steps," said Susan. "Jeffery, do let me be the first one."

"Certainly not," said Jeffery. "Those steps may look all right, but they may be quite rotten too. *I* shall try them first."

"Well, be careful, then, Jeff," said John anxiously. Jeffery stuck his torch in his pocket and sat down at the entrance to the hole. He tried the top step with his foot. With a crack it broke away at once, and the splinters went down below. Jeffery tried the next step." That broke too. The steps were as rotten as deadwood in a tree struck by lightning.

"Blow! The steps are no use at all," said Jeffery. "They wouldn't bear the weight of a mouse!"

"Well, how shall we get down then?" asked Susan, so anxious to explore underground that she simply could not keep still.

"We'll have to get a rope," said Jeffery. Both the others looked most disappointed at once. They couldn't bear the thought of going home and leaving the exciting hole even for an hour!

"Couldn't we jump down and chance it?" said John.

"Don't be so stupid," said Jeffery. "You'd break your leg to start with, and you'd never climb out again! Rags, go away. You'll fall in."

"Well, let's go home quickly and get the rope," said John impatiently. "Anyway, it's almost dinner-time. We'd better not be late again—though I'm sure we shall. We can come back after dinner."

"Come on, then," said Jeffery, and he turned to go. "Gracious! We *are* late again! Run!"

CHAPTER FIFTEEN

AN UNEXPECTED PUNISHMENT

THEY hadn't gone very far before a thought came into John's head. "I say," he said, stopping, "do you think we ought to leave that hole open like that? Suppose anyone came along and saw it—and got down before we did?"

"Yes—you're right, John," said Jeffery. "We ought to have thrown bracken and branches over it to hide it. Let's go back and do it quickly—it won't take a minute!"

But a great surprise awaited them as they made their way back through the trees. The sound of voices came to them!

Jeffery put his hand on Rags' collar at once, in case he should bark.

"Sh!" he said to the others. "Don't make a sound. Take Rags, John, and I'll creep up and see who it is."

Jeffery crept silently from bush to bush, keeping himself completely hidden—and at last he came in sight of the ruined building. He had a dreadful shock! Mr. Potts was there, with another man! They were looking in the hole and talking in excitement.

"Those children are smart!" said Mr. Potts. "They've found the very place. That map in the boy's pocket was wrong. We've been on a regular wild goose chase this morning, following goodness knows how many bends in the river! It's a good thing we heard their voices, and came to see what they were doing!"

"We'd never have found this by ourselves," said the second man. "This little hill is well-hidden, and the old building is fallen to pieces. Those are the steps shown in the map, Potts—no doubt of it.

But they're quite rotten. We'd better come back again with a rope."

"Well, those kids will be back after lunch," said Mr. Potts, rubbing his chin and thinking. "Let me see—how can we stop them? I know! I'll get my wife to phone up the old lady and invite the children to go for a picnic somewhere! Then they will be out of the way. I can't come back here after lunch, as I've business to see to—but we'll be here early in the morning before those kids are about."

"Well, come on then," said the other man. "I wish we knew a short way back—I hate wading in that marshy bit! I'm soaked to the knees!"

Jeffery couldn't help grinning. He wasn't going to show them the other way back! He waited until the men had disappeared round the humpy hill and then he shot back to the others. He told them all he had heard. They listened in rage.

" *Well!* " said Susan. "So he thinks he'll get the Treasure before we do, does he? He thinks he'll get us nicely out of the way for the rest of the day! Well, he won't. We'll refuse to go to the picnic!"

"Quite right," said John. "We've simply *got* to get here this afternoon. Then, when he arrives early to-morrow morning, he'll find nothing at all!"

"I say, we *must* go!" said Jeffery. "It's five to one! You know what a row we got into yesterday!"

They simply raced home, carrying the spades and fork, hoping that Granny wouldn't be too cross.

But she was. She was very angry indeed, and worse, still, Granpa was in a rage too.

"Half-past one! said Granpa, as they trooped into the hall. "Is that what you call being punctual? Two days running! Disgraceful! Really disgraceful!"

"We're awfully sorry, Granpa," said Jeffery.

"Being sorry isn't enough," said Granpa, looking really fierce. "Your Granny orders nice meals for you and then you keep the whole household waiting like this."

"It is really very naughty of you all," said Granny. "I've a good mind to send the dinner out and make you have bread and butter—but I'm sure you are all very hungry, and I don't like to do that."

"But you'll be punished all the same!" said Granpa, looking very fierce still. "Oh yes! You'll go up to your rooms after lunch and there you'll stay for the rest of the day. You'll have your tea up there and no supper! Bad children! I'm angry with you!"

Granpa stalked out of the hall and the children stared after him in dismay. What! Spend the rest of the day in their bedrooms, when they had such important work to do after lunch? They couldn't!

"Granpa!" called Jeffery. "Please forgive us. Just this once. You see . . ."

"I never listen to excuses," said Granpa. "You'll just do as you are told and say no more."

Susan began to cry with tiredness and disappointment. She stamped her foot. "It's too bad, it's too bad!" she shouted. "Granpa, you're unkind! You ought to listen to Jeffery."

"*Susan!*" said Granpa, in a shocked voice. "Don't be rude. I shall send you all up to your rooms immediately if I have any more nonsense."

Susan didn't want to make the boys lose their lunch, so she wiped her eyes and said no more. They went meekly into the dining-room and sat down.

"You mustn't make Granpa angry by arguing with him, Susan," said Granny, serving out big helpings of cold meat, potatoes, and salad. "You have really been very thoughtless, coming in late again like this, and you deserve to be punished. Now I don't want to hear a word from any of you. Eat up your dinner quietly."

Granny took up the paper and sat down. The children were very hungry indeed, and they ate quickly. Just as Granny had finished ladling out the raspberries and cream for pudding, the telephone bell rang.

The maid came into the room after a minute.

"Mr. Potts on the telephone, Madam," she said. Granny got up and went into the hall. The telephone was in the hall cloakroom. Granny left the door open, and the children could hear every word she said.

"Good afternoon, Mr. Potts," she said. Then she listened. "Oh, it's very kind of Mrs. Potts to offer to take the children for such a lovely picnic, but I'm sorry to say they can't come. No, they really can't Mr. Potts. . . . No, they are not ill . . . as a matter of fact, they have been rather naughty, and they have been told to keep to their rooms for the rest of the day. What? Yes—I'm afraid they will be indoors—they will not be allowed out at all . . . so you see they can't possibly go to the picnic—but please thank Mrs. Potts for me. Another day perhaps."

Then Granny listened again as Mr. Potts spoke for some time.

"Well, I'm glad you have really decided to buy Greylings," said Granny. "Yes—the papers will be ready for us to sign to-morrow. Our lawyer will be here, and if you like to come to-morrow morning at ten o'clock, the whole matter can be finally settled. Yes . . . yes . . . good-bye."

Granny put back the receiver. The children longed to speak to one another and say what they thought, but they had been told not to talk. Oh dear! So everything was to be settled at ten o'clock to-morrow morning. It was dreadful. Tears trickled down poor Susan's face and fell into her raspberry juice.

Granny came back. "Mrs. Potts wanted to know if you could go for a picnic with her this afternoon," she said. "Now you see what you have missed by being so silly!"

"I don't want to go picnicking with Mrs. Potts," said Susan. "I'm glad we're not going! I don't like Mr. and Mrs. Pots of Money!"

"Susan! Don't talk like that!" said Granny sharply. Mr. Potts is buying Greylings Manor, and you will have to be polite to him if you ever want to come and see the old place again."

"Granny! Please don't let him buy it!" said Jeffery. "Granny, we're going to find the Treasure for you, really we are!"

"Don't talk nonsense, dear," said Granny. "I suppose you are thinking of that old map? Well, I'm sure it doesn't mean anything at all."

"Oh, but, Granny, really we . . ." began Jeffery, but Granny wouldn't let him say any more.

"That's quite enough, Jeffery," she said. "Have you all finished? Well, go up to your rooms then. And remember that you are to stay there for the rest of the day. Tea will be sent up to you, but you'll have to go without supper—and I do hope you will remember that when you are guests in somebody's house the least you can do is to be punctual for meals!"

"We're very sorry, Granny," said John humbly, hoping that Granny would change her mind. "Couldn't we just stay in our rooms till tea-time and then take Rags for a walk?"

"Certainly not," said Granpa, who had come in at that moment. "I never heard of such a thing! Go along now—and can I trust you not to leave your rooms—or must you be locked in?"

"You can trust us," said Jeffery, his cheeks going red. "We promise to stay in our rooms for the rest of the day."

"Very well," said Granpa. "I trust you. The Greylings never break their word."

The children went upstairs slowly and sadly. They sat in the boys' room and looked at one another dolefully.

"This is the worst bit of luck that could happen!" said Jeffery. "Who would have thought that Granpa would be so fierce?"

"Well, what about Granny?" said John. "She was fierce too. And all the time we're trying so hard to find the Treasure for them."

"Yes, but grown-ups don't think of things like that," said Jeffery. "Oh, do stop crying, Susan. I can't think where you get all your tears from. I really can't!"

There was a scraping at the door, and Rags whined outside.

"The dear old dog!" said John, jumping up. "He wants to share our punishment too! Good old Rags."

Rags came in and jumped up on to Jeffery's knee. He licked the boy's chin.

"Jeffery, I suppose we can't possibly go to the woods?" said John, in a timid voice. "I feel as if we *must*—don't you think Granpa would understand, once we had got the Treasure?"

"I know enough of Granpa to know that he would rather lose the Treasure than have any of us breaking our word," said Jeffery. "We've given our word of honour, John, and we can't possibly break it. Don't even think of it! It would be an awful thing to do, and I'd hate myself for it."

"Yes—you're right," said John, in a miserable voice. "Oh, how I wish Mr. Potts was at the bottom of his own silly lake!"

That made Jeffery laugh. "That's where he tried to put *me* yesterday!" he said. "Well, old Pots of Money knows *we* are safely out of the way now, picnic or no picnic—so he's safe to attend to his business this afternoon. If only we could have borrowed a rope and gone down that hole—we'd have been down it by now if it hadn't been for this silly punishment!"

"I'm tired," said Susan. "I'm going to lie on my bed and have a nap."

But no sooner had she laid herself down than an idea came to her. She jumped off her bed and ran to the boys.

"I've got an idea!" she said.

CHAPTER SIXTEEN

AN UNDERGROUND ADVENTURE

THE boys looked at Susan. "What is it?" asked
Jeffery doubtfully. He didn't think there *could*
be any good ideas just at the moment.

"Well, listen, Jeff," said Susan, "We've promised
to stay in our rooms for the rest of the day, haven't
we?"

"Yes," said the boys.

"But we haven't promised to stay in them all night long!" cried Susan. "Mr. Potts is going to explore that underground place early in the morning—well, why can't we go *to-night*? We can take torches. We shall be quite all right. It would be just as dark down in that hole in the daytime as in the night, so it won't make a bit of difference, really."

"Well! That *is* an idea!" said Jeffery, really thrilled. "Why didn't we think of it before? Of course—we shan't be breaking any promise if we go there to-night. We'll go!"

"We'll go!" shouted John, and he banged his eiderdown so hard that the feathers flew out of it.

"We'll creep down Susan's secret stairs so that no one will hear us!" said Jeffery.

"We'll take our torches! We'll find a strong rope! We'll get the Treasure before old Pots of Money!" shouted John.

"Sh!" said Susan, delighted that her idea was thought so much of. "You'll tell everyone in the house what we're going to do if you shout like that!"

"I feel much happier, now," said John. "What shall we do till tea-time, Jeffery?"

"I think we'd better try and have a nap," said Jeffery. "It looks as if we shall be up half the night!"

So they all three lay on their beds and shut their eyes. The smell of the early roses outside the window came in. Bees hummed loudly. Everything was peaceful, and soon the children, happy again now, were fast asleep. They had worked so hard that morning, digging and scraping that they were really tired out.

They did not awake until Jane, the housemaid, came knocking at the boys' door with their tea. She came in and set the tray down on the table.

"And what have *you* been doing to get sent to your rooms like this?" she said. "Late for lunch, I suppose. There's nothing that makes your granpa crosser than that!"

"Oooh, what a nice tea you have brought us, Jane!" said Susan, looking at the tray of things. "Egg sandwiches—my very favourite ones! And what are these—potted meat. Thank you, Jane!"

"And ginger biscuits and seed cake!" said John. "Well, I shan't mind going without my supper now."

"You'll never be able to eat all this," said Jane. "Ring when you've finished and I'll fetch your tray."

"Thanks, Jane," said Jeffery. Jane left the room, and the three children drew up their chairs and began their tea.

They enjoyed it. They talked about what they were going to do that night. It was very exciting.

"I think we'd better keep slices of that seed-cake for to-night," said John. "We shall be awfully hungry if we go exploring at midnight!"

So they cut three enormous slices and put them in the top drawer of the chest. Then they rang for Jane.

"Good gracious!" she said, when she came in and saw what a lot they had eaten. "Nearly everything gone! *You* won't miss your suppers!"

She went, carrying the tray. The children found some cards and played Happy Families until seven o'clock. Then Granny came in.

"Well," she said, "I'm very sorry to have had to punish you like this—but you will please remember in future not to be late for meals, won't you?"

"Yes, Granny," they all said.

"You had better go to bed now," said Granny. "You are not coming down to supper. I will say good night—and I hope to-morrow you will turn over a new leaf, and we shall all be happy together again. It upsets me to have to treat you like this— but I promised your mother I wouldn't spoil you. You are usually such *very* good children!"

They kissed their Granny good night and listened to her going down the stairs to the hall.

"It's not worth while getting undressed," said Susan.

"Yes, we'd better," said Jeffery. "Granny may come up again for something—or even Granpa—and we don't want to get into any more trouble. We can easily dress again about midnight."

So they undressed and got into bed. But none of them could go to sleep! They talked to one another and listened to the hall clock chiming the hours and the half-hours.

"Granny's gone to bed now," said Susan. "I heard her door click. It must be eleven o'clock."

It was. The clock struck eleven almost at once. The children talked again until midnight—and then, when the hall clock chimed, they slipped out of bed.

"Don't make a sound," said Jeffery. "If we drop anything on the floor it may waken Granny or Granpa."

So they were very quiet indeed. They were soon dressed. Jeffery took the slices of cake out of the drawer and they all ate them. The cake tasted delicious at that time of night!

"We had some supper after all, said John, with a grin.

They took their torches, and opened Susan's cupboard. The top of her secret stair was there and one by one they crept down the tiny winding stairway to the dining-room. They crept out of the dining-room and went to the garden door at the side of the house. It was locked. They unlocked it and stepped outside.

"Good! There's a bright moon," said Jeffery. That was lucky. The moonlight lay on the ground like pools of silvery water, and everywhere was bright.

"Where is Rags?" asked Jeffery. Jane had taken him down with her at tea-time, and he had not come back.

"In his kennel, I expect," said John. So they went to the kennel and there was Rags, staring at them in delighted astonishment. What! A walk at this time of night! Well, he was quite ready for it! He slipped out and joined the children.

"Now for a rope," said Jeffery. They went to Tipps' shed and shone their torches round. They soon found that there was quite a big coil in one corner. It was thick and strong, just what they wanted.

Jeffery picked it up. It was heavy. He flung it over his shoulder, and thought he could carry it quite easily like that. Then, with Rags at their heels, they set off for Timbles' Farm, for that was the shortest way to the ruined building.

They had to use their torches in the wood for it was dark there. They arrived at the hole, and pulled away the branches and bracken that covered it. Mr. Potts had put them back, for he did not want anyone else to find the hole.

"I'll go down first," said Jeffery. He tied the rope to a tree-trunk nearby, and then let the other end fall down the hole. Then he let himself carefully down the rope, swung on it, and slid down slowly to the ground below.

"Come on!" he shouted to the others, flashing his torch around. "There's a passage here. It smells a bit musty, but it's all right—not blocked up, or anything."

The other two slid down the rope. Jeffery helped Susan, who was so excited that she might have fallen. They all three switched on their torches and looked around.

In front of them was a narrow passage, with the roof just above their heads.

"I believe it leads into that hill!" said Jeffery. "You know—the little humpy hill."

He was right—it did! The children followed the passage, which was very narrow in parts, and at last came out into a curious oblong room, hewn out of the very heart of the hill!

It was strange to stand there in the light of their

torches, and look round at a room where no one had been for many, many years.

"This must have been a hiding-place for the Greylings at some time or other," said Jeffery. "In the old days people were often ill-treated because of their religion, and maybe this room was a hidey-hole for long-ago Greylings. It's a marvellous place—right in the heart of a wood—and in the heart of a hill!"

"Where is the Treasure, do you suppose?" asked John, looking round. They flashed their torches everywhere. The room was furnished very plainly with strong wooden benches and an old narrow table. On a shelf old plates and mugs still stood, dusty and cobwebby. The floor was tiled like the floor above. There was no fireplace at all.

"I can't see anywhere for Treasure to be hidden," said Jeffery. "I say! Wouldn't it be too disappointing to have come all this way, to the very end of the map, and find that the Treasure wasn't here after all!"

"Jeff, look—there's an old wooden door in that corner," said Susan suddenly. She shone her torch there and the boys saw what she meant. They had not noticed the door before, because the walls were of earth and the door was as brown as the earth.

"I say! I wonder if that's a cupboard or any-

thing!" said Jeffery, in excitement. He went over to
the door. It was fast shut, and seemed to be bolted
on the other side.

"Funny!" said Jeffery. How could it be bolted
the *other* side. People wouldn't bolt themselves
in a cupboard surely!"

"The door is as rotten as those steps were," said
John. He aimed a kick at the lower part of the old
door. It gave way and the wood broke at once.
John kicked again, and soon there was an enormous
hole in the door!

Jeffery put his hand in at the hole and felt about
for bolts. He found them but they were too stiff
to undo. So he and John kicked at the door until
it had almost been kicked away, and the three
children could easily squeeze through the hole.

It wasn't a cupboard. It was the entrance to
another passage, a little wider than the first one,
and leading in the opposite direction.

"Come in—let's see if we can find anything here,"
said Jeffery. He walked a few steps and then came
to a stop. In his way, stopping up the passage, lay
a great wooden box, with bands of iron round it.
The lock had rusted, and the lid was loose.

The children shone their torches on it and looked
at one another, very thrilled. Was it—could it be—
the Treasure, at last?

B. C. FREEMAN.

CHAPTER SEVENTEEN

THE TREASURE AT LAST !

"I HARDLY dare to lift up the lid in case the box is empty!" said Jeffery, in a whisper. Nobody knew why he whispered, but it seemed the right thing to do. He lifted up the lid—and then, oh what a marvellous sight!

The Greylings Treasure lay in an old box! Somehow or other the dust and the damp had kept away from the box, and the Treasure shone undimmed. Great brooches, wonderful necklaces, jewelled pins— and loveliest of all, the wonderful Greylings cup made of pure gold, with its handle and the middle studded with precious stones! Jeffery lifted it out.

"Look!" he said. "Oh, look! The very cup that we saw pictured in that old book. The lucky-cup! It's been here for years and years and years. Oh, what will Granny say? She'll be rich! She won't need to sell Greylings after all!"

Susan began to jump up and down in excitement. She forgot that the roof was so near her head and she jumped right into it. But she was so happy that she didn't even feel the bump. She knelt down by the box and put her fingers among the jewels.

"Pearls for Granny! Brooches for Mummy! Lots of lovely things for everyone," she said. "Oooh! This is wonderful! How clever we are, aren't we, Jeffery?"

"I think we are rather," said Jeffery. "After all, people have been hunting for this lost Treasure for years and years—and now three children have found it!"

"Won't Mr. Potts be angry when he hears that we got here first and found everything!" said John. "And he'll be angrier still when he finds that Granny won't need to sell her dear old house to him after all! Oh! I'm longing to get home and wake up Granny and Granpa and tell them everything!"

"Listen," said Jeffery suddenly. "What's that noise?"

They all listened. "It's Rags barking," said John, in surprise. "What's he barking at?"

"Suppose somebody is coming through the woods," said Susan, clutching Jeffery. "Suppose it's Mr. Potts and the other man, coming at night? What will he say when he finds us here?"

Jeffery ran back into the oblong room, and then made his way down the first passage. He shone his torch up to the top of the entrance hole. Rags looked down, wagging his tail. He gave a short yelp.

"Is there somebody coming, Rags, old boy?" said Jeffery. "Come on down with me. Jump!"

Rags jumped into Jeffery's arms. He was very glad to be with his little master. Jeffery listened and at last heard something. It was the sound of people scrambling through the wood! In the silent night the sound could be heard very clearly.

Jeffery thought quickly. There was no time to get out. Was there any good hiding-place up the second passage for them? Could they take the Treasure with them and hide it? But how could they carry that heavy box?

He took out his pocket-knife and cut a good piece of loose rope from the rope that hung through the hole. It might be useful. Then, hearing voices coming nearer, he shot back to the others.

"Sounds like Potts and one or two more," he said. "Come on. Let's see if this passage has got any sort of hiding-place for us."

"How are we going to take the Treasure with us?" asked John.

Jeffery quickly tied the rope round the big box. He knotted it at the top, leaving two long ends, which he looped firmly. He gave one loop to John and took the other himself.

"We can carry the box between us," he said. "It's too heavy for one person—but we can easily carry it like this, swung on the rope."

"Good idea," said John. "Get out of the way, Rags, old boy. You don't want this box on your head!"

Susan had crept to the old room and had listened to see what was happening. She heard somebody at the entrance to the hole.

"Hallo! Look here!" came Mr. Potts' voice. "Somebody's dropped a rope down. I didn't see it this morning, did you?"

"No," said another voice. "I suppose those kids aren't down there now, are they?"

"They'll be sorry for themselves if they are!" said Mr. Potts, in an angry voice. "Making false maps and trying to throw us off the trail—stupid little idiots!"

Susan waited to hear no more. She fled up the second passage to tell the boys.

"Oh, here you are," said Jeffery impatiently. "We wondered where you were. Don't go disappearing like that just when we've got to escape."

Susan told the boys what she had heard. The three of them set off up the second passage, the boys carrying the box between them.

"I only hope this passage *leads* somewhere!" said Jeffery. The underground way ran straight for some time then turned to the left. It was dark, musty, and low. The three torches threw a bright light in the dark tunnel.

The passage suddenly split into two ways—one to the right and one going straight on.

"Blow!" said Jeffery. "Which way ought we to go, I wonder?"

John anxiously shone his torch up first one way and then the other. "The right-hand way seems a bit wider," he said. "Let's go that way."

"Right," said Jeffery. "Susan, have you a handkerchief? Well, throw it down on the ground just a little way up the *other* passage, will you?"

"Whatever for?" asked Susan, in surprise.

"So that old Pots of Money will think we've gone up that way, and follow the wrong path," said Jeffery.

Susan laughed. "You *are* clever, Jeffery!" she said. She threw her little white handkerchief down on the ground a little way up the passage. Then the three of them, with Rags nuzzling against their legs, took the right-hand tunnel.

It went on for ages. Once they came to where part of the roof had fallen in, and had to climb over a heap of stones and earth.

"I feel like a rabbit running through a burrow," said Susan.

"With foxes behind us," said John.

"Oh, don't!" said Susan. "I hope Mr. Potts has gone up the wrong passage."

Mr. Potts had! He and his friends—there were two of them this time—had jumped down the hole, found the strange underground room, and squeezed through the broken door that led up the second passage. But when they came to the splitting of the ways, they caught sight of Susan's handkerchief, just as Jeffery had hoped they would.

"They've gone up there," said Mr. Potts. And up the wrong passage they had gone! But before they had gone very far the passage came to an end in a small cupboard-like room, whose walls were of stone. It was quite empty, though, hundreds of years before it had been used for storing and hiding many things.

By the time that Mr. Potts and his friends had turned back and gone to follow the children's passage, the three treasure-finders had got a long way ahead.

"I simply can't *imagine* where this is leading us to," said Jeffery, putting down the box for a moment. It was really very heavy, and though the two boys were strong, their arms were aching badly.

They went on again after a bit. Rags ran ahead, thinking that all this was a fine adventure! Every time he turned round his eyes gleamed like the head-lamps of a small car, in the light of their torches.

Suddenly the passage came to an end—and facing the children were a few rough steps of stone.

"Hallo—look at this!" said Jeffery. "We've come somewhere at last."

John shone his torch overhead. The stone steps led to a square stone slab that lay flat in the earthy roof above their heads.

"Why, it looks as if there's a slab of stone at the entrance here, just like the one we moved," said Jeffery.

"But not nearly so big," said John. "Get up the steps, Jeff, and try to heave up the stone with me."

Both boys went up the steps. They bent double and heaved with their backs against the slab. It seemed to move a little.

"Jeffery! John! They're coming! I can hear them!" suddenly cried Susan. "We shall be caught. Oh, do hurry!"

There was the sound of voices and footsteps to be heard a good way along the passage. Jeffery and John pushed at the stone slab with all their strength. Rags ran back along the passage, barking loudly and fiercely.

"That's right, Rags! Keep them there! Don't let them pass!" shouted Susan. Rags felt grand. He tore down the passage till he saw Mr. Potts and his friend and then the plucky little dog stood in front of them, barking, growling, and showing his teeth. He would *not* let them pass!

The children heard Mr. Potts' voice shouting to them.

"You naughty children! What are you doing here at this time of night? Call your dog off. He's making himself a nuisance!"

The children didn't say a word. Jeffery heaved up with all his might—and the roots of the grasses that had been clinging to the stone slab and keeping it tightly in place, all gave way. The stone lifted up—and Jeffery put his head out into the cool night air!

"Golly! It's open!" said John, thrilled. "Just in time too! Come on, Jeff—hand out the box. Susan, come along. Leave Rags there to bark and give us a start!"

The children all climbed out of the hole. They stood there in the bright moonlight for a moment, wondering where they were. And then Jeffery suddenly knew!

"We're near Timbles' Farm!" he cried. "Look— there it is, down there, beyond the field-gate. Do you know where we are—we've come up inside that funny little ruined stone hut we saw the other day in the field. We wondered what it was! Fancy! There's an underground way between the old building in the wood and this one—and we've found it!"

"Oh, do come on," said John, who was very much afraid of being caught. "Let's go down to the farm and wake Mrs. Timbles up. She'll look after us!"

"Come on then," said Jeffery, thinking it would be very nice to see plump Mrs. Timbles. They half-stumbled, half-ran down the slope of the field, the boys still carrying the box between them.

When they came to the pig-sty, Jeffery put the box

down. "Let's hide the Treasure here," he said. "Nobody would guess it was in a pig-sty!"

The others giggled. It seemed funny to hide treasure with the pigs—but as Jeffery said, no one would ever think of looking there!

So under the straw of the pig-sty went the old box. The pigs grunted sleepily in surprise. Jeffery stood up and stretched his tired back.

"Look! There are Mr. Potts and friends," he said. "Let's go and wake the farmer! I feel as if I'd like a grown-up on our side now!"

CHAPTER EIGHTEEN

SAFE AT TIMBLES' FARM

IN the bright moonlight the children could see the three men running over the sloping field. What the men were going to do the children couldn't imagine —perhaps they would take away the Treasure— perhaps they would be very angry indeed—they might march them all the way home, and tell some dreadful story to Granny and Granpa.

"Come on, let's bang on the farm door," said Jeffery. "No one will find the Treasure in the pig-sty."

They ran round the farmhouse, and Jeffery banged on the big knocker there. The sound thundered through the night. Crash! Crash! Crash!

A window was flung up and the farmer looked out in astonishment.

"Who's there?" he shouted.

"It's us!" shouted back Jeffery. "We're in trouble —somebody is chasing us. Let us in!"

"Good gracious—it's the Greylings children!" said Mrs. Timbles' voice, and her head appeared by the side of the farmer's. "I'll go down and let them in, Fred."

In half a minute the big bolts were being drawn back, and the great wooden door was opened. The children pressed inside and Jeffery banged the door. He could see the three men coming up the path.

"Now, my dears, what is all this?" said Mrs. Timbles, in the greatest astonishment. She looked very queer because she had on an enormous white nightgown, with a pink shawl thrown over it, and her hair was done up in four tight plaits that stuck out round her plump red face.

Before the children could answer there came

another knocking at the door. Mrs. Timbles jumped.

"Bless us all!" she said. "Who's that now?"

The farmer came into the hall; he had pulled on his breeches, and put on some bedroom slippers. He looked just as amazed as his wife.

"Fred! There's someone at the door again!" said Mrs. Timbles.

"Ay! I can hear them," said the farmer. "I'll open before they knock my door down."

The children went into the big kitchen with Mrs. Timbles. She lighted the oil lamp, and poked the fire which still showed red.

"Why, you're shivering!" she said, looking at them "You can't be cold this warm night."

"We're shivering with excitement," said Jeffery. "Oh, Mrs. Timbles, take care of us, won't you?"

"Of course, of course," said Mrs. Timbles, in still greater surprise. "You're safe here."

The farmer brought Mr. Potts and his two friends into the kitchen. Mr. Potts looked very angry. He glared at the three children, who stood close to fat Mrs. Timbles.

"Now what's all this about?" asked Farmer Timbles, looking sternly at the three men. "Have you been frightening these children?"

"Let me explain," said Mr. Potts. "I have bought Greylings Manor, and . . ."

"You haven't bought it yet!" said Jeffery.

"Don't interrupt, my boy!" said Mr. Potts. "The final papers are being signed to-morrow—but I regard myself as the owner of Greylings lands now. Everything is settled."

"Well, what's all that got to do with you being out at this time of night?" asked Farmer Timbles.

"My friends and I are interested in the old ruins belonging to Greylings," said Mr. Potts. "Naturally those belong to us, as well as the house and grounds. Well, we have beeen doing a little exploring, and these children have very strangely and rudely been trying to interfere with our affairs. My friend here is an authority on old books, china, jewellery, and so on, and I have promised to let him have any old Greylings property to examine."

"You're not telling the story truthfully," said Jeffery, boiling with rage.

"My dear boy, don't be rude," said Mr. Potts. "As you can see, Farmer, these children are quite out of hand. Well, we have been looking for some old things that belong to the property—and we have reason to believe that these children have stolen them to-night. This is a very serious matter, Farmer, as you will see—but if the children are willing to hand us back our property now, we will not make any more trouble about it."

"They didn't bring anything in here with them at all," said Mrs. Timbles. "And let me tell you, sir, that these children are not the sort to steal! I never heard of such a thing!"

"Mrs. Timbles! It was the Greylings Treasure we found!" said Jeffery. "It's Granny's and Granpa's! It doesn't belong to Mr. Potts. We found it to-night! They were after it too—these three men!"

"The Greylings Treasure!" said Mrs. Timbles, in the greatest surprise. "Well, I never did! The Greylings Treasure! Are you sure, Master Jeffery?"

"*Quite* sure," said Jeffery. "We looked it up in an old book, and saw the pictures of some of the things —and they were there, in the old box!"

"Well, my boy, you must let us have the box," said Mr. Potts. "I tell you, I have bought Greylings, and anything found on the property is mine. You will get into serious trouble over this, if you don't give me what belongs to me."

"That's so," said one of the men.

"I don't care!" Jeffery almost shouted. "You shan't have it!"

"Well, Jeffery, give us the box to put somewhere safe just for to-night," said Mr. Potts. "Then to-morrow we will all go into the matter with your

Granny and Grandfather. You will see that I am right. Now, be a sensible boy and tell us where you put the Treasure."

"Well, lad, I think maybe you'd better do that," said Farmer Timbles. "If this gentleman *has* bought the property, you'd better be careful."

"I will *not* give up the Treasure!" said Jeffery.

"No, we won't!" cried Susan and John. They were all quite certain about that.

"Then we shall find it ourselves," said Mr. Potts, looking furious. "And you will get into trouble, all three of you. I'll see that you do—you interfering little wretches!"

The men went into the hall and out of the front door. They began to hunt about in the moonlight for the box of Treasure. The children flew to the window of the front room and watched them. Would they look in the pig-sty?

They did go to it—but the sty smelt and the men didn't even open the gate. They did not think for one moment that the children would have chosen such a peculiar place!

Mr. Potts suddenly grew tired of the search. "Come on," he said to the others. "We'll have something to say about this to-morrow!"

To the children's great delight they saw the three men going away. Then, and not till then, did they pour out their extraordinary story to Mrs. Timbles and the astonished farmer.

Jeffery and John went out to the pig-sty to get the box. It was covered with straw, and did not smell very nice—but who cared for that! How the children enjoyed Farmer Timbles' surprise when they opened the box and displayed the marvellous things inside! Mrs. Timbles too, could not believe her eyes. She would not even touch the things— she just stared and stared at them, saying, "I never saw such a thing! Never in my life!" over and over again.

"So, you see, we've got the lost Treasure at last!" said Susan, jumping round the kitchen like a frog. "Isn't it awfully exciting, Mrs. Timbles?"

"I never heard of such a thing!" said Mrs. Timbles, and her plump face looked even redder than usual with the surprise and excitement.

"Well, I'm going to take you children back home," said Farmer Timbles, getting up.

"Oh, couldn't the little things stay here for the night?" said Mrs. Timbles. "They'll be tired out."

Jeffery did not at all like being called a little thing, but he was so delighted at the thought of staying the night at the farm, that he felt he didn't mind anything. The children looked at the farmer anxiously.

"Well, let them stay if you want to," said Farmer Timbles. "I'm not wanting to dress and go out at this time of night! We will telephone to the Manor early to-morrow morning, before the children are missed."

So that night the children cuddled down in soft goose-feather beds at Timbles' Farm. They were terribly excited and terribly tired—but very, very happy. They didn't care what Mr. Potts said—the Treasure was theirs!

CHAPTER NINETEEN

GOOD LUCK TO THE GREYLINGS !

THE children's grandparents were immensely astonished when the telephone rang early the next morning, and the news was told them. At first they simply couldn't understand it—but when they heard Jeffery's voice on the phone, telling them that he had found the Treasure, the two old people sat down and stared at one another in astonishment.

Farmer Timbles told his wife to give the children some breakfast, but for once in a way the three were really too excited to eat anything. They swallowed down the creamy coffee that kind Mrs. Timbles made, and then begged the farmer to take them home in his pony-cart.

They were afraid of meeting Mr. Potts on the way home! They wanted to get the Treasure safely to Greylings Manor. So Farmer Timbles put the fat brown pony in the little cart, and brought it round to the front door.

He and Jeffery put the box in the cart. Then they said good-bye to Mrs. Timbles and climbed into the little cart themselves. It was a bit of a squash but nobody minded.

"Gee up there!" said Farmer Timbles, and the pony trotted down the farm lane. "Clickitty-clack, clickitty-clack," went her hooves.

Granny and Granpa were waiting excitedly for the children. They really couldn't believe it was true! They had telephoned to a friend of Granpa's, an old man who was very wise about long-ago things, and knew whether they were real or not.

He had arrived just before the children came. His name was Mr. Frost, and his hair was as white as his name. He, too, was very excited, for if the children really had the old Greylings Treasure, it was very wonderful.

The pony-cart clattered up the drive. The children sprang out, and the farmer lifted the old box on to his shoulder. Granny opened the front door and the children rushed to meet her.

"Granny! We've got the Treasure!"

"Granny! We've had such an adventure!"

"We've found the Treasure, Granny!"

"What a noise!" said Granny, and she led the way to the study, where Mr. Frost sat talking to Granpa. Granpa had got out the old book that showed the Treasure, and he and Mr. Frost were examining the pictures carefully.

Farmer Timbles put the old wooden box gently down on the table. "It's been in the pig-sty," he said, with his large smile. "I'm afraid it doesn't smell very good."

Nobody minded that! Granpa flung back the lid and everyone looked inside. For a moment there wasn't a sound to be heard. Then, to everyone's surprise, Granny began to cry! She cried quite quietly, and the tears rolled down her soft pink cheeks one after another.

"What's the matter, Granny?" asked Susan, in alarm, putting her arms round the old lady.

"Nothing, dear—just tears of happiness," said

Granny. "It's so wonderful—just as we were thinking of selling Greylings, you find the Treasure!"

Mr. Frost looked quite amazed. With his long thin fingers he took first one thing and then another out of the box. Soon the table was covered with precious jewels, and the wonderful golden cup shone in the midst of them.

"Yes," said Mr. Frost, in a low voice, "yes! This is all old—very old. Wonderful stuff. Marvellous! And to think it has remained unspoilt and undiscovered all these years!"

"Is it worth a lot of money?" asked Susan.

"It is worth a fortune!" said Mr. Frost. "It is almost priceless! This cup alone is worth thousands of pounds."

"Ooooh!" said the children, and looked with wide eyes at the dull gold of the carved cup, with its precious rubies and sapphires shining and glowing around it.

"But I shan't sell this cup," said Granpa. "The famous Greylings cup, found after so many years! It is unbelievable! The lucky-cup is back where it belongs!"

"Granny, you won't have to sell Greylings now, will you?" asked John.

"No, we shan't said Granny. "We shan't have

to leave our dear old home—it will be your father's—
and yours—and your children's!"

"Mr. Potts said that it was his, last night," said
Jeffery. "I knew he wasn't telling the truth."

"Well, he almost was," said Granpa. "Except for
my signing one document, and Mr. Potts signing
another, the sale was completed. I'm not sure even
now that we shall not have some difficulty in
drawing back from the sale. We shall see what our
lawyers say. I have no doubt that we shall find
a way out all right."

"It seems to me that this man's strange behaviour
will not sound too good when it is told to your
lawyers," said Mr. Frost suddenly. He had listened
very carefully to all that the children had said. "I
think, my dear sir, that you will find Mr. Potts will
not want anything said about his behaviour, and
will not make any more trouble."

"He did make Jeffery fall into the lake," said
Susan. "We are sure of that."

"Yes. He is not a charming friend to have at all!"
said Mr. Frost. "I shall be interested to hear what
he has to say about all this."

Susan, who had been listening impatiently to all
the talk, suddenly went quite mad! "But we've got
the Treasure, the Treasure, the Treasure!" she
yelled, dancing round like a top. "Nobody can

take that away from us! It's ours, it belongs to the
Greylings! Hurrah! Hurrah!"

She took up two pearl necklaces and hung them
round her neck. She pinned two enormous brooches
to the front of her frock. She put an enormous
bracelet round her wrist, and took the golden cup
into her hand.

Everyone watched her and laughed.

"*I've* got the Treasure! *I've* got the Treasure!"
she sang, and danced round the room again. Just at
that moment the door opened, and Jane showed in
Mr. Potts and his lawyer! Susan almost bumped
into them.

Mr. Potts stared at Susan in amazement when
he saw all the jewellery she wore. "The Greylings
Treasure!" he said. "So you *did* find it after all! I
began to think last night, when we hunted round
the farm for it, that you had made up the tale of
finding it, just to annoy us!"

"It was in the pig-sty, the pig-sty, the pig-sty!"
chanted Susan.

Mr. Potts suddenly remembered Granny and
Granpa and bowed stiffly to them.

"I have brought my lawyer to hand you my
cheque for Greylings," he said. "And, Mr. Greyling, as your property is now mine, I also claim the
Greylings Treasure."

The children held their breath. What would Granpa say to that?

Granpa offered the box of cigarettes most politely to Mr. Potts. "I'm afraid," he said, "that there will be no sale. I can't accept your cheque, as now that the Treasure has been found, there is no need for me to part with Greylings Manor. I very much regret that you have been put to so much unnecessary trouble. I shall be pleased to pay you whatever sum our lawyers agree upon to make up for the trouble you have been put to."

"But this won't do, this won't do!" said Mr. Potts, in a rage. "You can't get away with things like that! I'll soon show you that you can't behave like this to me."

"Mr. Potts," said Granpa, in a voice like icy cold water, "if I have any nonsense from you, my lawyers will hear my grandchildren's tale of your very peculiar behaviour this last week—and I do not think you would want that make public. I quite understand your disappointment over the sale—and over the Treasure—but I do feel very glad that Greylings Manor is not going to belong to your family! I think, if I may say so, that it deserves a better fate!"

Mr. Potts listened to all this with a furious face. He went red—and then white—and then red again.

He tried to speak. He swallowed hard. He looked as if he were going to burst—and then, with a noise that sounded like the squawk of an angry hen, he stamped from the room. His lawyer followed him, looking worried.

The front door banged. There was the noise of a car being started up. It sounded as angry as Mr. Potts had looked.

Then the car drove off down the drive. Everyone heaved a sigh of relief.

"Horrid man!" said John.

"I feel rather guilty about him," said Granpa. "The sale *was* almost completed—and I would have considered myself bound to go on with it, if it had been any other man. But I have heard such strange tales about Mr. Potts lately that I feel he is not the right owner for Greylings—and now that I have heard how he has scared you children, and tried to get the Treasure for himself, before the sale was really completed, I am glad we have defeated him!"

"Oh, Granny! Oh, Granpa! Isn't everything lovely!" cried Susan, who was still wearing a great deal of jewellery. "Oh, I'm so happy! Greylings belongs to Greylings—and we can go on coming here as often as we like!"

"You certainly can!" said Granny, hugging the